A Slice of Trust

A Slice of Trust

Yashobanta Samal

Translated by
Harekrushna Das

BLACK EAGLE BOOKS
Dublin, USA

 BLACK EAGLE BOOKS

USA address:
7464 Wisdom Lane
Dublin, OH 43016

India address:
E/312, Trident Galaxy, Kalinga Nagar,
Bhubaneswar-751003, Odisha, India

E-mail: info@blackeaglebooks.org
Website: www.blackeaglebooks.org

First International Edition Published by
BLACK EAGLE BOOKS, 2025

A SLICE OF TRUST
by **Yashobanta Samal**

Translated by **Harekrushna Das**

Cover & Interior Design: Ezy's Publication

ISBN- 978-1-64560-737-3 (Paperback)

Printed in the United States of America

Foreword

Yashobanta Samal is one of those few storytellers in Odia who portrays the society around him with a sharp sense of humanity without loading the stories with heavy philosophical speculation or abstraction. The world as he surveys is not an ideal world; it is inhabited by people of all sorts of character who seem to be moving somewherearound us. Their honesty, simplicity, hypocrisy, follies and foibles constitute the warp and woof of the fabric of his stories. The characters with their commonplace attributes seem one amongst us; a familiar friend who has grown up with us; or an acquaintance next door or asimple folk we come across in our daily life whom we look up to with awe, wonder, ridicule, compassion and humour.

The stories move as the characters grow up to unfold their traits, layer by layer, and take the readers by surprise and unexpected turnof events. The storyteller doesn't thrust upon the readers any idea about the characters, but when he does so, as an omniscient narrator,the characters appear familiarly human through their actions. The stories in the present collection offer vast canvas against whichdiverse facets of society have been portrayed with realistic values and appeal. The storyteller metamorphoses his characters into touchstones that judge the masked people moving around them, dissect their emotions and intentions, and expose the hypocrisy which has been wrapped up with gentility. Be it the simple tribal girl, Kurei or the rebellious Sukanti living in the Kaibalya, the society of the so called elites - they all have been used by the writer as mirrors who faithfully reflect the concealed social reality. Interestingly, Kurei remains wordless throughout the story whereas Sukanti is a verbose reactionary who exposes the social hypocrisy through her keen observation and expert judgment. The portrayal of the society becomes even more intensely realistic when the writer's omniscient narrative undertakes a microscopic analysis, of the pseudo-gentility of the men and women of the present society, with a ruthless sarcasm.

The activities, interactions, discussions and deliberations of the women of the Kaibalya Society are so amazingly depicted with a touch of peculiar feminine realism, humour and satire that the readers can visualise the characters as ones that are familiar to them and moving around with a bearing of truthfulness.

Even the stories of a relatively shorter length are treasures of irony, satire and humour in as much as they expose the hypocrisy of people who dupe others with their pseudo personality. 'Kurei' humorously brings out the dichotomy between words and intentions in such away that even the narrator is not spared. He speaks words ofsympathy to his wife asking her to engage Kurei in her householdchores, but his intentions of deriving pleasure by seeing the girl for alonger time can be clearly perceived as the writer describes differentactivities taken up by men only as plea to enjoy the sight of the girl.

The hypocrisy of leading a contented conjugal life is pitifully exposed in the 'Monkey's Heart.' The age-old tale of monkey-crocodilefriendship finds a surprising parallel in a modern context. Most peopleput up a show of conjugal happiness even though their original heartis already stolen and secure with someone else. They continue toproject a false smile of belongingness before their spouse and theworld so that the marital harmony is maintained. Through such anironic existence of human beings, the story exudes an essential truth of life: happiness might be an illusion, but illusion needs often to be maintained to keep one happy.

The writer is also quite critical of the modern society that values only appearances. In 'Photograph', he mocks both the head clerk and the officer who do not bother in the least about the sincerity of helping people during Corona. Only a photograph that displays the gesture of helping is all that matters to them. The overtones of mockery in this story subsides as the writer dwells upon the psychological impact of staying locked down at home for a longer period of time. The people who are accustomed to spending time outdoors are the worst victims of Lockdown. The memory of such people are so severely affected that a person is unable to realize his identity even until ten minutes of conversation. The narrative is entirely humorous and satisfying.

Humour of course presents an aura of refreshing energy to the stories, but Samal artfully fuses with it elements of pathos and seriousness in order not to let the stories appear light. Despite all elements of humour and satire, the stories like A Slice of Trust, Horse, Gedu and The Undying deal with serious issues and are psychologically revealing. The small boy who earns his living by selling egg rolls, in the story, A Slice of Trust, is looked upon by a gentleman as one who should not be trusted, but the boy himself exhibits a kind of humanity by giving out a packet of egg rolls as a gift. This gesture of the boy is certainly a blow on the pseudo-gentility of modern human beings. On the contrary, the friends of the speaker whom he looks up to with absolute trust are the ones who slaughter his trust.

The implied irony in the title itself brings out the intent of the author in dealing with social issues and human relations. Human emotions and filial obligations are callously sacrificed by the modern generation in order to climb the ladder of material success. Bunu's utter apathy and insensitivity towards his parents and his paternal house not only shows the moral degradation and rotten values of the contemporary society, it also brings out the dehumanizing effect that money does produce in the present generation. The old couple - Aditya Babu and Usha Devi - are of course helpless; pining for the love and comfort that they could find in the company of their son, daughter-in-law, and the little grandson but such pleasure is a far off dream for them, they know. Aditya Babu, therefore, tries to find happiness in the company of Khusi (literally meaning, happiness), the little child of their tenant. But plot hatched by the daughter-in-law conspires to snatch even that happiness. Such is the irony of existence.

Samal's essential vision of life is not a bleak one, but he believes that happiness truly is an illusion. Thrust into this dark and unsatisfying world, man thirsts for happiness. And, happiness in this modern world is defined by sheer materialistic possession and prosperity. Thirst for such happiness is insatiable. Therefore the rise of cheats and impostors posing as merchants of happiness. The subtle irony and sarcasm used in the story 'Thirst' reveals the futility of searching for happiness in a world outside, while it actually dwells in one's heart, in the feeling of contentment.

Such feeling of joy and contentment can be generated in

the heart even by sacrificing one's own pleasure and interest. It is not easy to fathom what lies beneath the appearance of a person. The narrator is taken by surprise to find that compassion, sympathy, love and a sense of sacrifice moistens the heart of the seemingly uncultured Gedu. And no wonder, hatred, hypocrisy, treachery, and insensitivity hides under the elite appearance of the Kaibalyaites. Truth always remains submerged, like an iceberg, under the deceptive surface. Samal uses irony, humour and sarcasm to expose the reality. This is what makes his stories distinct and pleasing.

Apart from the judicious selection of the subject, the craftsmanship woven into the stories leaves the readers in awe. The storyteller juxtaposes characters of sharply opposing nature to bring out the distinction more brightly. The characters move along an unpredictable course until the storyteller makes a surprising revelation to drive home the ultimate message. This comes with the reversal of the readers' expectations. The message becomes clear, but the story does not end; it leaves an eternal dissatisfaction in the heart of the readers, and an insatiable desire to know about the final outcome of the narrative. This feeling of dissatisfaction is truly a great feature of agood short-story. The stories in the present collection will definitely amuse, entertain and stimulate the readers. The collection will hopefully gather a wide readership.

Harekrushna Das
Translator

CONTENTS

A Slice of Trust

He did not ask anything today. When he saw us approaching his stall, he only smiled. And began to prepare rolls. He would normally ask on other days, "single or double eggs, Sir?" or would say, "Delicious chicken pakoda, sir. Please take it. I would refund the money if you don't find it tasty." The businessman-like words that did not suit his age - he had just stepped in his teens - were very pleasing to hear. He would often bang his spatula on the cooking pan to make a ding-dong sound and attract customers, and would shout - "the special item today... chicken free with egg roll."

One of my friends who was there with me after his office hours surveyed the environment with his sharp eyes like a detective agent, and raising his nose up to his forehead he asked, "you take egg roll from here?" Then his eyes instantly stretched up to the stinking drain flowing with murmur at the back of the stall. Keeping his hanky pressed on nose remarked that I did not have a taste. Besides that I did not have the elementary knowledge of health consciousness. Toestablish his opinion he hinted at me to look at the boy and asked, "does he have gloves in hand and chef's cap?"

The boy had cautious ears for our conversation, and smiled at us intermittently during his work. That innocent smile of his was a great attraction for me. A smile springs up from my lips whenever I see him smile. I have never bothered to think if has or not gloves and cap. My friend dragged me to a little distance. He was getting amused by satirizing my sense of health awareness. Besides, he wanted to prove that I had no knowledge about an important matter, for which he dragged me by my hand up to the bike. With a show of his experience and prudence he said, "the intent of the boy doesn't seem good! Don't you notice how he acts cunningly, like a thief? His eyes are fixed on the pan, but ears are alert at us. Just see how surreptitiously he listens to our words. Thieves have very sharp eyes cast in all directions - two eyes in the front and two at the back."

I looked at my friend's face with surprise. He seemed to be beaming at my foolishness and ignorance. He could discern from the wrinkles created on my forehead, and my quiet gaping that I was doubtful of his opinion. To remove the fog of suspicion from my mind he tapped on the dickey of his bike, and asked, "do you know where is its key? Can guess it?" No lock was there, the key-hole was tied instead with a piece of plastic string. Unable to guess anything I asked how that had happened. "Mischief of these boys." Raising head from above the dickey he hinted at the boy making egg roll; and his eyes became smaller with their corners getting squeezed as a result of some deep thought." Do you think that these people earn their living by making egg rolls? This is only an outward show. Behind this, they have unfair trade. And yes, never tell them your identity and address. Be cautious... There was frequent thefts of fuel from vehicles in our colony"... Making his voice a bit muffled he looked at the boy. The boy had been making roll along with the tune of a song he was humming. My friend felt relieved that our secret discussion had not reached the ears of that boy, and then resumed. "We guarded the colony in turns, and finally nabbed the thieves. The two miscreants looked almost like this boy. We thrashed them heavily and handed them over to police." My friend was grinding his teeth in such a way as if the thief was standing before him, and he was pronouncing his judgment for the culprit. He secured his dickey with two more knots on the string tied to it, and patted the seat of the bike with great satisfaction-there it is. I was listening to my friends narrative with gaping mouth. The way he narrated the episode would make anyone believe it. Gift of the gab is one of his distinctive qualities. Given the chance, he can unhesitatingly sermonise for hours. Audience would gather around him and disperse, but he would never feel tired. Another unique character of his is that he undertakes almost a research while buying grocery and vegetables. No seller can ever deceive him, but mine is a different case. I have absolute trust on the shopkeepers, and therefore have to listen to my wife's chastises, "would anyone with eyes bring such rotten brinjal? Did anyone give these fruits for free?" But, my friend is one unlike me. Even if purchases a toothbrush, he would minutely examine brushes of at least five different companies to verify the length, design, and if it has adequate bristles to clean the molars properly. The fading manufacturing-date, the free gifts if any, the disclaimer (by the company) written on the packet in extremely small letters that are straining for eyes - all these things also come under his close scrutiny. Another of his specialties is that he can forecast, even by observing the mere packaging, if a company will go bankrupt in five years or will prosper significantly.

It is very usual on the part of a person who is able to

judge the quality and standard of a number of companies to doubt the credibility, honesty, quality, cleanliness and price of "Friends Roll-Maker." "These people are actually not what they seem!" He said pointing his fingers at a row of vendors-on-wheel. "One such boy used to sell mixture at the market square near our colony. Just as a little intimacy developed between us out of our regular interaction, he once appeared at home pleading in tearful voice for lending him one hundred rupees as he needed it go home to see his ailing mother. I was reluctant but agreed when my wife persuaded. Already four months gone where is the money?" The boy had already indicated twice with his hand that the packet of rolls was ready. My friend's speech was unwilling to end, but he concluded with a tip, "stay on your guard; these people cannot be trusted." He whispered these words, into my ears, like a gospel which the boy didn't have any chance to overhear.

Regardless of my friends sermonisation; misfortune was never to quit me. I suddenly realized, and became sure, that I hadn't brought the wallet today. I had forgotten it in some other pants at home. How shall I pay thirty rupees to the boy? I fussed once again through the pockets of my pant, but nothing more could be found than a mere hanky. Seeing me flustered my friend expressed his doubt with a grin, " Did you forget your wallet at home?"

"Oh, yes. Please give me thirty rupees. See, what a humiliating situation." I stretched my hand towards my friend for help. He threw a sardonic smile at my helplessness, and said, "You are exactly like me, quite forgetful. I have also several times, come across such situations that you are in today. This is very common; take it easy." He fled away with his bike but not without expressing his annoyance, "Have to take my daughter to her tuition. Already late: you delayed a lot by gossiping." I kept fussing through the empty pockets of my pant, as if I had been itching with the touch of some poisonous plant, and looked helplessly at the road. I was hopeful that I would definitely meet some friend who will rescue me out of this awkward situation. But alas!

What an absurd law of the universe! The man whom you meet every day would never turn up on the day you need most. What would the boy be imagining about me! He might be thinking that the man is so poor that he does not keep even thirty rupees in his pocket. He might even take me for one among those cheats who appear honest and pretend to have forgotten wallet at home and promise to pay sometime later.

Oh! The pain is too much to bear. The nearby shopkeepers, a few young men and women gathered around the stalls now began to throw deliberate glances at me. I should have checked my pockets before giving orders for rolls. Why did I act foolishly! Ah! While I had been abusing myself writhing with the pain of an unseen wound, I could hear a well-known voice from behind, "Rakesh Babu!

Looking dejected!"

Just as a surge of happiness springs from the heart getting transformed as a smile when the solution to a problem is suddenly discovered or at least the clue to the solution is found, I was overwhelmed with such a feeling when I saw Mishra Babu. I wouldn't have felt so much joy if I had met him at some other place or time. I hugged him with great delight. I do not know how he took my over-enthusiasm, but looked up to him as an angel who has descended upon this earth to rescue me from a crisis.

We were working in the same office some five years ago.

He got transferred to Balasore with a promotion, but his family continued to live here. "And, how are you, dear?" Mishra Babu started off his talk with a friendly query "How much do you gain with this new pay- commission? They cheated us this time. There was a handsome hike the last time." He continued with his lecture without waiting for my reply, and abused the government like anything. He was annoyed that salary did not increase proportionately for all categories of employees. I was at that moment unable to think of the pay commission. Neither had I calculated how much I would gain with the new salary.

I always feel that how so much the salary might increase, the middle class people are always in scarcity. The rate at which the market is going dearer, one's pocket turns empty by the twentieth day of the month irrespective of how much one earns. With this kind of self- consolation, I have refrained myself from all calculation. Mishra Babu is not the kind of man who would slacken; he keeps record of every minute detail. "Huh! This government has already made us stifled levying taxes upon taxes! Have to pay tax even with a cup a tea!" Mishra Babu continued with his speech in his peculiar manner. He seemed greatly excited seeing me after a long time; and began to broaden the scope of his speech. With the kind of situation now in America, our children..."

I interfered with his speech, and whispered into his ears. "Give me thirty rupees, please. I am in a very awkward situation now." He looked at me with a clear indignation as if I was an idiot. Where is America.. or pay commission... but I asked him for thirty rupees! Shit! However, he tolerated my arrogance, and a smile bloomed on his lips as if he had forgiven me, and then said with a concern that matched my worry? "Oh! But, I am sorry. I have no change. I just withdrew a two-thousand rupee note from the ATM. Going to get some change at the Petrol pump." He went away with his scooter abusing the government for introducing the two thousand rupee note.

With his going away from my hand's reach, my last hope moved away from my hand's reach. I came away with embarrassment from the stall, and made my eyes swim across the road. And again fussed through my pocket lest some miracle might happen. Observing my worriedness, the boy called out to me from his stall, "Sir! Please come here, sir!" I decided not to take away rolls today with a plea, but as I had been thinking of concocting a plea, the boy consoled me, like a wise old man, with smile on his lips, "Why so much worry, Sir? Perhaps thinking of not taking away the rolls as you have forgotten to bring your wallet. Isn't it? But I'll definitely pack these rolls today, and request you to convey your daughter, my Didi, that this is a small gift from a younger brother for her on her birthday."

Surprising! How did the boy come to know that today was my daughter's birthday? Was my friend correct then in his assessment? Unable to hold back my suspicion, I asked, "How did you know that today is her birthday?"

He displayed a kind of smile on his lips that a student radiates on his lips while coming across very easy questions. "Hadn't Didi, madam and you been to the temple this morning? I work in the morning at the stall where you bought materials for worship. I sold flower and earthen lamp to Didi and Madam this morning. I learnt from their conversation that today is Didi's birthday." I was looking at the boy with consternation. Taking notice of my reluctance to accept the packet of egg rolls he said, "We are staying in the slum near your colony; my brothers are vending snacks and momo at the other end of this area. Please wish my Didi Happy Birthday on my behalf, Sir." With these words the boy now stretched out his hand with the packet of rolls towards me.

A slice of guileless smile dangled from his lips with an indication that an earthen lamp of trust, reliance and heartiness still glowed somewhere inside the bounds of distrustful and calculative relationship. Words carrying a tone of blessings, sprang from my lips, "What is your name, dear?"

Kurei

Kurei. Everybody here knows her by this name. She reaches our colony by the time the crow caws in the morning. Her job here is to sweep houses, clean utensils, and wash clothes of the Memsaabs. With the beauty that Kurei has, she could surely have secured at least a class-III govt. job if she had only studied a little or was born in cities like Cuttack or Bhubaneswar. But to her misfortune, she was born in some obscure hamlet of Kalahandi where cooking hearths do not have the opportunity on most days to get fire burning inside, and where many people think that Bhawanipatna is the best town in the world.

Except a few slum-dwellers in the colony where I have been staying for the last six months, all the residents have been staying on rent. Kurei works as a domestic house cleaner at residences of ten or twelve Saab's from among these tenants. Her job is just like the routine of a school; it starts in a new house as soon as she finishes it at one house. Whenever Kurei goes to the roadside tube well to fetch drinking water, a group of teenagers wearing jean pants and singing modern film songs at the nearby market square stare at her with hungry eyes.

Even the eyes of the unyoung tea seller swims from his

stall up to Kurei. The Saurindra Babu, Barik Babu and Viswanath Babus who browse through the morning newspaper sitting at the porch, and order their wives to bring hot tea as it has already become cold actually deceitfully go on flipping the pages of the newspaper only to prolong their surreptitious looks up to the tube well. I also make best use of this opportune hour, while having a shave at the rooftop, to be amused, and excited with all this spectacle woven around Kurei.

"Shall I ask that girl to come and help you with your domestic chore?" I just proposed to my wife the other day. "Which girl?" She questioned with a little smile but greater suspicion.

"Don't know that girl?... O, I just forget her name... the girl working at Sumanta Babu and Prakash Babu's residence...?" I never uttered the name to be Kurei even though I clearly remembered it.

"O... that girl!" She reacted in such a manner that it seemed as if I had suggested bringing some terrible object to our home. "O no, no. Don't you worry at all. I don't have really much to toil at home.

Have I ever asked you to bring a house cleaner that you show so much concern? I am perfectly alright." She went inside the kitchen cutting me short.

I knew my plan had failed, but since it would not be wise to speak anything more about it, I kept mum with silent grumble. The main topic of discussion among the assemblage at the market square was Kurei's growing youth, her candid talk and outright behaviour. I have observed experienced people whispering words of wisdom into the ears of the less experienced ones describing the shapes of Kurei's limbs, the parts of her body that are enticing and enjoyable - I feel infuriated at these people; these scoundrels don't have the least sense of courtesy ! Is Kurei a public property?

Anyone can stare at her the way he pleases, pass remarks, give hints, or even fancy about the Kinds of revelry that can be done with her carrying her to some secluded place! I also sometimes consider myself guilty as a number of unparliamentarily questions about Kurei pop up in my mind, and vent out from my mind in a gush of sigh. I feel very uncomfortable at such times. One morning, the sound of the tube well could not be heard. Everybody became worried. Someone informed that Kurei was absconding. The congregation at the market square seemed greatly frustrated, even greater than one would seem when some heavenly object moved away from one's hands' reach. The gentlemen who used to put up a show of browsing the newspaper were observing quietude; their newspapers lay neatly folded without any possibility of being opened. I was vacillating whether or not have a shave. The Kurei-centric people were in observance of an undeclared national mourning.

A few days after this incident, my wife told me one night, "It becomes very strenuous to do all the domestic chore. That girl had come this evening. I have asked her to come to work from tomorrow." Sleep suddenly absconded from my slumbering eyes. "Who came?" I asked trying to keep my curiousity suppressed. "O, that girl, Kurei. She has got married in the meanwhile. Her husband is perhaps a driver. You had been to the market when she came today." Even though I believed the news of Kurei's return, I was not prepared to accept the news of her unanticipated marriage. But since any discussion on this matter with my wife was not out of danger, I decided to wait patiently till morning.

Crow cawed heralding morning. The morning of a new century. The market square once again reverberated with the sound of the tube well. I rushed to the rooftop with the shaving kit in my hand. Kurei's getup had changed. Tucking saree in her waist, and wearing it above the ankles, she carried water to the houses. She glistened brighter than ever in the tender sunrays of the new century. She seemed ever more fragrant just like the Kurei flower. Moreover, the vermillion dazzling on her forehead like the bright sun made her beauty even more entrancing. And, there was an astonishing change in the spectacle from that day. Veterans, little experienced ones or novices no longer thronged the market square. The Babus in the habit of reading newspapers now did it sitting in their drawing rooms. I announced no more to go to the rooftop in the plea of severe cold out there. However, my wife looked greatly delighted today, more than that was expected of her.

Monkey's Heart

Not any ordinary monkey she was. Doctors were only informed that she was the inamorata of the monkey who had kept his heart hidden in the hollow of a tree-trunk. Eight surgeons along with the chief surgeon were all ready for this rare kind of surgery; and all arrangement had been made to present to the viewers all across the globe, the live telecast of the process.

With advancement in age, the lady has developed certain complications with her heart, for which an open heart surgery is the only solution; and, therefore, this arrangement is. Doctors and nurses present in the operation theatre are all agog with excitement. They all had read the story in their childhood, and still remember it with numerous recounting, that the monkey had been able to befool the crocodile and escape. Here, this is the ladylove of that very same monkey !

The chief surgeon moved the scalpel, and screamed-"Oh my God...!" The assistants leaned forward to get the view inside the bosom and exclaimed as if in a chorus -"Oh my goodness... how is it possible!" Two dozens of small hearts, like a bunch of grapes, were nestled in the place of the heart. Each one was active and had a peculiar symbol on it.

The doctor picked a heart from the bunch. It had written on it the English letter 'A'. No one could decipher anything of it. But the eminent merchant, Anadi Charan, who was at that time enjoying himself in his drawing room with a cup of tea, was startled - that one was his heart! The girl for whom he used to reserve a seat in the Chakadola bus keeping his hanky on a seat while commuting to college some twenty years ago, had stolen this heart of his, and had disappeared thereafter! Ah...!

The doctor picked another heart from the bunch; its plump body had written on it the letter 'S'? Soumya Ranjan Das, the Administrative officer, could recognise it as he watched it on the TV screen. While studying M.A, both of them had made the croton plant in front of the Coffee House almost bald by regularly plucking all its leaves. White plucking the leaves, she had also plucked this heart of his; and had then disappeared...!

The chief surgeon took out twenty two hearts, one after the other, fifteen large-sized, two mediums, and five small-sized ones which the donors were able to recognise watching them on the TV screen. Among the ones who identified the hearts were the bookstore owner - Ramaballabh, the medicine Store owner- Ajit, Sana bhai -the fruit vendor, Rankia Uncle-the bicycle mechanic, Rashid-the Postman, professor Panda, Mahanta - the taxi driver, the manager of Rocky hotel...

All of them got absent-minded as they recognized the precious thing of their own. When the wives noticing the absentmindedness of the husbands, wanted to know the reason, the husbands simply asked to switch off the TV saying it was showing an old episode on the Discovery channel. The team of surgeons was astonished when they observed, after picking out the whole bunch, that the patient did not have a heart at all.

When, left with no other way, they had stitched the empty bosom, the patient immediately ran away.

A kind hearted surgeon suggested to the chief surgeon, "Sir, how would it be if we sent each of these hearts to their owners? Place an advertisement?"

"Are you mad?" Screamed the chief surgeon, and said," The real owners are now living happily wearing duplicate hearts. Do you want to destroy their families !!" Each of the young surgeons present there stealthily caressed their bosom trying to feel if their heart was beating or not, if it was original or duplicate?

The chief surgeon tried to explain the mystery to the stupefied young surgeons, "Listens guys none of us possesses our real heart. while swimming across the river of time, we cannot know when someone steals the thing from us. Whether in the tree-hollow or in a vanity, it lies with some other one. Just think of me....."

Photo

Artta babu had been loitering in front of the gate for an hour with a pair of masks in his hand. He has become frustrated after waiting so long - where are those two lanky guys! They turn up every day at eight in the morning, but no sign of their coming today even though it is nine o'clock now! Useless guys.

Almost everyone in the office, except Artta babu-the Head clerk, have already uploaded photos. The boss has ordered - " All of you please exhibit humanitarianism during this period of the pandemic, Corona; discharge your social responsibility. And post photos of your magnanimous act in the WhatsApp group of our office." Artta baba is quite experienced, conscious, and efficient, too. Twenty-five years have already passed with such a character of his. Studying the files thoroughly, analysing and understanding the matter clearly, discussing it the with the beneficiaries - he moves the files onward unhurriedly and carefully. If someone questions his slow pace, he would explain - this is the matter of survival of a person; handling it hastily may cause errors.

So, naturally, he delayed a week to post his photo. But,

the Whatsapp group of the office was teeming there with photos and videos. Photos of giving food to monkeys at Khandagiri, water to bulls near Lingaraj temple, bundles of straw to cows, distributing soaps at the Tarini slum, and photos of serving lunch with tear- brimming-eyes to beggars at the station square. The kind hearted boss, trying to encourage the employees, was generous in posting comments - 'thank you, well done, keep it up' and a thumbs up. Certain excited young employees had sent even four or five photos.

Artta babu was watching and reading everything; but was still cuddled up with inaction; the government issues several such orders, and also forgets everything in a few days. Why should he be so hasty ! But his colleague, Prabir, spoiled everything when he wrote - "Artta Sir, how are you? Stay home, stay safe" What was the need to write such things in the group! Idiot, a trickster!

Where are those Kalu and Bhola, now!! All tension will be over once I make them wear these masks, and upload its photo. The boss will be pleased, and I will be saved from the attack of those rogues. Artta babu has never been on good terms with Kalu-Bhola. Arguments and bickering everyday. Artta babu, as such, is a sincere person apart from being a member of the Conscious Citizens' Committee. So he always keeps vigil on Kalu-Bhola. "Hey... you two... why don't you move the brooms with a little force? will it cause pain to the road or to you both? You are piling the leaves over there... who will set fire to it, eh? When will you remove that rotten coconut tree-trunk... six months have already gone since the last cyclone... where is that drain-cleaner? He has not turned up this week... should formal invitation be sent to him."

Bhola doesn't say anything, but Kalu answers back; he is

not one to be cowed down. "Listen, Sir. Our duty is only to sweep, and not to clear the rotten tree trunk or to clean the drain. You should speak to the contractor; he has asked us to sweep two more roads. Are we human beings or machine?" Artta babu would shout as kalu answers back, "Hey! How dare you argue, answer back! Do you know who Arttatran Satapathy is?

You will see; I will lodge a complaint against you today. You will be dismissed from here. Hmm! After all, we are paying tax; why shouldn't we speak out! You think you will cheat us, eh ?" Such quarrels are quite common in the first week of every month. Almost everybody gives some tips of ten or twenty rupees to these two sweepers. Artta babu, as such, is a conscious citizen; he would not give them a pie, but would surely teach them certain tricks. - "You should complain at the Municipality office if the contractor doesn't provide you with slippers; his license will get cancelled.

Have you formed an association or not? Got me or not?" That same conscious citizen, Arttaballabh, loiters today to welcome Kalu-Bhola as if they were his guests; and holds the masks in his hands in a manner that befits worshipping. As scratch-sound could be heard, he raised his head to throw a look at the bend of the road. A thoroughly vacant road. A few stray dogs were parading within the boundary of their territory. They were also in a state of doubts and apprehension - where are their masters today? All that was there was the music of the cuckoo, and chirping of birds. No trace of humans, making scratch-sound, Kalu- Bhola were coming as they were sweeping the road. They were moving forward with harmonious steps, like the marching of soldiers, as if they were going to a war-front.

"Oh, Bholanath! Kalandi! Please do come, guys." Such

a pleasant address by Artta babu created doubts in the mind of the guys. Unable to believe it, they looked here and there. As it was usual on his part, Artta babu should have raised his brows throwing a suspicious look at these two. But, which direction did the sunrise today in! When they noticed masks in Artta babu's hand, and his getting the mobile phone ready for a selfie, they could understand the motive behind his pleasant words. A number of officials have already taken selfies making them wear masks and throwing gamcha around their neck. A few enthusiasts have even wrapped flower garlands on their neck, as if they were scapegoats! The same matter of photo is the reason for their one-hour-delay today. They can't say 'no' to anyone. The guys of the Youthclub, corporator, members of the temple- committee whoever met them on the way, made them wear masks, and took selfies. Even though it was hypocrisy and a forced situation, pleasant words can at least be heard, people are coming to stand close to them considering them humans, at least. Were they ever able to get such opportunity from the gang of these gentlemen!

Artta babu suddenly realized to have landed in a dilemma. The matter had not occurred to him earlier; but everything will turn hellish now! He will have to put the masks on the faces of those sweepers in his own hand! What is to be done now!! Unable to think of a solution, he stood dumbstruck for a while. The sweeper-guys could decipher the predicament that Artta babu was in, and said, "Sir, we no more need a mask now. We have already worn one, and have five more with us. If you need any more, you can take a few from us. But kindly click a photo soon, and let us go; we still have other streets to sweep!" With these words, they posed themselves for a photo, with the long handle of their broomsticks tucked in their hands, like guns.

Artta babu felt liberated. Maintaining a social distance of six feet, he stood to the right of one of the sweepers, and got the camera of the mobile phone ready for a selfie. "Oh, yes... raise the brooom a little upward. Ok, there... right hand on the mask... near your left ear.. smile... click!" He uploaded the photo without the slightest delay, and captioned. "A Step Towards Awareness."

His luck, as such, is quite bright; the boss instantly reciprocated a comment - "Thank you, well done, keep it up..."

"Oh my God! At last..." A deep sigh flew away from the bosom of the sincere and conscious Arttaballabh.

Illusion

Satyabrata had stretched his intent gaze standing on his balcony towards the rows of tree on either side the road lying in his front. The effulgence of colours that the Goldmohur and Palash flowers strewed under the morning sunrays seemed as if the procession of lights accompanying the band party of some marriage party has paused here on the way. And, the beauty of the moment was made even more delightful by the enchanting melody of a bird. That enthralling music came flowing from amidst the dense leaves of the verdant bower nearby.

The bird had already made Satyabrata absentminded since quite some time, but he was not able to identify which bird it could be that emanated such an enticing music. The voice seemed quite familiar of course, but he could not recollect the name of the bird. He was not able to see the bird. It seemed, as if the former girlfriend was making a phone call from an unknown number hiding herself at a distance !!

Reliving the pictures of the village of teen and early adulthood days! And, Lo! Here it flew away. Ah! How beautiful with intense yellow hues! Oh no! This is Golden Oriole! He was quite sure that such a melodious voice could not be that of on Oriole. Now the bird began to sing with an even higher pitch as if challenging Satyabrata to recognise her; challenging his memory.

A senior executive in an insurance company, Satyabrata is now in doubt. The man who is able to explain lucidly the philosophy of life, and life after death to audience of all ages and captivate them with his talk, and two-times winner of the Beemashree Award- Satyabrata is now nable to recognise the voice of a bird! Oh! The name now slips away from the lip of the tongue! Oh!. Not any insurance policy is there that Satyabrata is unaware of. Everything is at his finger-tips. If a person tells him only his gender and age, he can immediately suggest which policies would be beneficial for that individual. He can even list out at a breath the names of about twenty policies like Jeevan Jeevan, Jeevanrang or Jyotishree that are either dead or dying. And, benefits in different policies, which ones produce early return, the ones that are profitable during lifetime, which ones bring more profit upon death, more bonus- generating policies, a list of alive and dead customers, who have benefitted from particular policies, along with their address - he is capable of recounting everything in details without making a mistake, but now he is unable to recognise a bird! How could he forget this sweet voice in these few days of Lockdown!

Twenty-one days already gone, nineteen more days are there to be waited. Complete shut down due to Corona. People are confined in their homes. Market closed, shops closed, no plying of vehicles, betel shops closed, no playing cards, no rendezvous. If you step out towards the market, police would thrash you. So, Satyabrata was loitering from inside the bedroom to the balcony, and again from the balcony to the bedroom just to move up his legs that have turned stiff. The brain has also begun to become dull after so many days of sitting idle at home. Divine symptoms that befit saints have also begun to appear. It was a matter of only yesterday. Seating his wife beside him, he started preaching her sermons about the mundane affairs of this ephemeral world, citing a couplet from the Bhaagabat, and said,

"You see, everything is illusion; everything is transient." But the wife could decipher a certain thing, and said, "All this ranting is the result of not being able to smoke cigarette and join the rendezvous. Keep your sermons reserved for some other time; now, just get up and clean the smut from the ceiling with the broom; I am going to mop the floor. Why do you meddle all day and night with that mobile phone? Leave it first! Why don't you watch the Ramayana or the Mahabharat on the TV? Huh! Came to give me sermons...!"

The bird again started to sing. This time it seemed to have perched quite closer. Wiping the lenses of his spectacles, he moved his eyes searching through the dense leaves and branches of the mango trees. And now flew away two birds. These were perhaps those singing birds. Perched so far joyfully in the quietude of the dense leaves, like a newly wedded couple. Satyabrata suddenly remembered that a profitable policy had just been launched for the newlyweds- Puspit Jeevan. Endowment policy, has good return. A slice of smile flashed on his lips. He looked gleefully at those birds, flying in a circular motion, to wish them congratulation. The bird-couple accepted the wish and congratulation, and reciprocated by twittering. Oho! These are sparrows. That sweet music can never be of these two. Satyabrata once again became lost in his world of thoughts.

What could be the name of that queen of music? What an enchanting voice! "Hurry up, Papa! You have to bring chicken. All the shops will shut down by ten. It is already 9.30. When will, you go?" The cute little daughter shook her father by arms, and brought him back from the world of birds.

An aura of irritation enveloped Satyabrata's complexion. He had been imbibing a unique experience after quite a long period of time; the daughter spoiled his meditation "What? Chicken! Will you eat chicken on Thursday!!!" There was a marked annoyance in his voice, but he immediately consoled, "I will surely bring it on Sunday. Ok, my sweetie?" He caressed the head of his daughter, and again cast his look along the road. But, the daughter was not one to quit. She said, "Who told you that today is Thursday? Today is Sunday. How do you forget it?" Satyabrata was startled. "What! Today is Sunday!" He was sure that it is Thursday today. He lovingly explained to his daughter, "Since your school is closed, you have forgotten the dates and days. No worry; you just go and ask your mama to make tea! Caressing her head once again, he kept looking at the mango tree.

It was now the turn of the daughter to be struck with surprise. Patting her palm on her forehead, she said, "Papa, you quite often forget your key and spectacles, but now you have started to forget days and dates ! Ok, come on with me, let's verify it with the calendar." The little girl tried to drag her father by his hand. Satyabrata's phone began ringing when the little daughter was searching the calendar. He joyfully started the conversation, - "Hello, Binod. What's up, where are you now?" "Hey, I am not Binod. It's Ramesh. Are you busy right this moment?" -"Ramesh! Oh, I'm sorry, I have taken off my spectacles; so I couldn't see your name correctly.

I'll tell about me later. You first tell about you. Is everything right or not?" -"I had sent you a song sung by Laxmi. Did you listen to it? She has sung it well."

"When did Laxmi become a singer? That was by Pallishree. Have you started to develop the disease of forgetting? ha ha...ha..." "Oh, yes. It was Pallishree." Ramesh sounded apologetic, and continued, "You are right. Why such things happen these days, I can't understand. Names, cases-everything is getting slapdash these days..

A certain client phoned me yesterday. I tried a lot to make it out to him, "Listen Das babu. Nothing can now be done for your GIA case. Offices closed; court is also closed. So, please keep patience." The gentleman revealed after ten minutes of conversation, "Sir, I am Patnaik babu and not Das babu. Mine is the divorce case; not a GIA case."

The bird, just at that moment, once again saturated the whole environment with the sweet music of its voice. Satyabrata once again become oblivious. "Hey, Satya!" Ramesh tried to shift the topic. " Are there cuckoos near your house? Singing so sweetly! Have you built a bower over there? Ha ha" Just as Satyabrate listened to his friend's jest, his eyes became wide open with a realization. Cuckoo.!! Oh yes-yes. It is cuckoo for sure. A smile of contentment spread on his lips. When the father was nodding his head repeating Cuckoo...

Cuckoo..., the little daughter stomped towards him with the calendar in hand, and showed it to her father with her finger, "See it here, Papa; it is Sunday today... nineteenth of April. No more excuse will do now...huh..." the pampered girl sat, making swollen face, clung to her father. Satyabrata now smiled at his daughter, but he could not recollect what his little daughter was pleading for.

Gedu : The Silent Love

When I opened the door with my eyes still sleepy, it was Gedu. The sleep of about an hour or two was still left. Since it gets about twelve or one in the night while going to bed, to get up late has become a habit. Sleep as such becomes a little more deep in Sunday morning; and if anyone presses the door bell at such hour, it is quite obvious to be greatly irritated.

Before opening the door I thought that it must be the dear flower- thief. While hooking flowers, buds, and even twigs, the hook must have fallen on this side. Now with the plea of discussing the world affairs, he would slyly pick his hook and go away. This has happened many times previously; there will be no more leniency. But see, here is Gedu! Trying to exhaust on him all the anger for the flower-thief, I began, "My dear Gedu; everybody knows whatever you do, and wherever you go; now you chose me to..." An unparliamentary word stuck to my throat while getting slipped. I suddenly noticed a lady standing behind him! Now all sleep from my eyes, anger from my head and words from the mouth instantly vanished. "O Pundit! Will we go back from here or you will invite us to get in?" Gedu took his bag off his shoulder as he displayed a line of familiar stained teeth. A reluctant smile tinged with disbelief, fear and apprehension cropped up in my lips - "Oh, yes, yes. Please do get in." Gedu got in carrying his airbag, and followed suit the lady as she bowed twice before me with namaskar. Just as he got inside, Gedu showed everything to the lady, as if it was his own house - this is drawing room, bedroom over there, and this one is the kitchen. No one else is here; the Pundit stays alone in the aashram. No need to be bashful of anybody here.

The bathroom is there at the outside. Refresh yourself quickly. consider it your own home; we are chatting up here. What a strange man! No information, nothing else; but appeared along with a lady! Gedu is of course not married; but he has a lot of scandal in his name in the village. He was earlier a womaniser, endowed with such art of Krishna; but now he is perhaps into this business. "Hey bood buck! You don't have any sense of honour, respectability or shame; but if the police enters my house while searching for you, I will first be arrested. Will my fame that is growing up as a pundit and renowned astrologer ever remain untarnished? And my income? Who will then come to my rescue if my family lands in trouble?" Gedu is my childhood friend. Three years older than me. Has studied with me up to class eight.

There were many similarities and intimacy between us. Firstly, no one in the school ever called us by our good name. His name in the register was Trilochain Jena, but everybody called him Gedu which literally means a dwarf. He was of course not a dwarf, but was smaller in comparison to his age, and was the smallest one in the whole class. My name was Gananath Das. I was the tallest one, and was called Dengu which literally means a tall one. I was happy when friends called me Dengu, the image of Amitabh Bachchan, the tall filmstar, flashed before my eyes. We were popular as Dengu-Gedu pair. The second similarity was, we both were extremely poor at studies. I of course managed to secure some marks more than he did, but everybody, not only in our class, but in the whole school had known us as donkeys. But we did not have the least sorrow or regret to have obtained the title of 'Donkeys' ; it rather made us get closer.

We used do sit together on the last bench. Although Gedu deserved a seat on the first bench considering his height, the class teacher granted him a special permission to sit beside me lest the bright students should get infected with his dullness if they came in his contact. To have been seated on the last bench was quite a delight for us. When the teaching gains momentum in the class, Gedu would elbow me and signal me to concentrate upon the girls on the first and the second bench and shove in my hand a few balls of paper prepared with great care. Pratima Nayak always keeps looking with all attention and concentration at the teacher's face as if she would gulp down everything that is being taught. She is very beautiful and a good student. Ruby, Ankita and Daisy would look back at us and smile when our paper-balls hit them, but Pratima alone never looks back. Gedu's aim is infallible. The paper-balls hit her back like petals of flower, and roll away; she doesn't still look back, nor does even lodge a complaint. I cannot ever hit my target, but the mission is carried out so cautiously that no one can ever identify the real hunter. Gedu never loses hope, rather elbows me with a confidence and smile, and says, "Pratima will someday definitely turn back and smile; just wait with patience." I cannot help laughing at his words. "You keep on dreaming, dear Gedu. Pratima has in the mean time already talked with me twice."

I was a good singer. Gedu wanted to learn music from

me. But since I was not a music teacher, it was decided that he would listen to me singing, and learn it. We leisurely pass time at the mango orchard by the river bank, and enjoy the scenic beauty and the activities going on before our eyes. The wave of Kaashatandi flowers, murmuring song of river Mahanadi, the unmissable hunting by the Kingfishers, the crane moving wavily - like a king - saddled on a cow's back, the chorus of bells tied around the necks of the cattle, the diffusion of colours of the setting sun in the sky, the maidens laughing heartily at the bathing-bank and the mothers admonishing them... a romantic song spontaneously flows out of my throat as I witness this canvass and effulgence of colours. Gedu keeps looking at me intently till the end of the song. I feel encouraged as I observe Gedu's rapture and start singing another song. Gedu tries to imitate me as I conclude singing, tries a lot straining his throat but in vain. Gedu plays on the flute brilliantly. Be it devotional song, modern song, Hindi song, Odia song or folk song - he can play the tune of every song. Anyone would halt to listen to his flute. He played his favourite tune so melodiously that the whole world eagerly listened to the music. I also loved the same. I wanted to play flute like him.

He taught me how to hold the flute, how to move fingers, and other things, but everything in vain. He could not learn singing, nor could I play flute, but our unison became a matter of discussion in nearby villages. Some people appreciated it mentioning it as the blessings of God whereas the teachers predicted otherwise, "these two are lost cases; far away from studies, they will not be able to read any more!" We could not actually study properly. Both of us failed the exam of Standard-8 securing almost the same marks. A great concernment rent our family; there was a lof of discussion, and analysis, trying to find the cause of this disaster. And everybody concluded, as in a chorus, that this condition of the dear boy is the consequence of bad company. And as a remedy, I was transferred to the Govindpur School which was four kms away.

When I announced to Gedu the sad news of having failed, I thought he would weep or seek my advice with a sorrowful heart as I had scored ten marks more than him. But his reaction surprised me. He became so much happy, and laughed that even the student who came out first in the class would never have become so much happy. He pulled a packet of bidi from his left pocket, and a matchbox from the right, and exploded, "Oho! A great tension is gone... let's stroll towards the mango orchard." Gedu's family- condition is despairing. No farmland of their own. His father cultivates other's land on lease. His elder brother, a matric-fail, doesn't ever step on to the mud of the farmland. Now a personal help of the MLA, he dreams of doing a job at Bhubaneswar. Gedu has two sisters younger than him. The entire family survives on the toil of the parents. It was as if necessary that Gedu should fail in the exam at such a crucial period of the family, and Gedu had eagerly been waiting for this moment. " What will you do now?" I asked doubtfully

-"Will be a helper" he replied with confidence

-"Helper! But where?"

-"Daulat Singh! The Samantaray Company. I have settled it. Fifty rupees daily besides fooding. Salary to be increased later. A helper has extra income, too; you can't understand it. I can send at least one thousand rupees to my father. An old man he is, how long can he toil?" Patting me on my back, he said, "You carry on your study; study a lot, be a Collector. I am not able to satisfy my stomach; how should I study? Ha ha ha" He puffed out a whirl of bidi-smoke with a careless horselaugh that seemed to quaver the mango orchard. The day marked the end of the song-flute symphony. If at all it could be heard, It was only once or so in a month. But, who is this lady? Gedu has never told me anything about her. I have been worrying with the thought of police since the moment they entered my house quot;Hey, Do tell me who she is. Is this the same lady whom you had been talking about two months ago? Is she from Bhadrak of Balasore?"

Gedu didn't give a reply. He went away as if he couldn't hear me, and handing me a cup of tea he had made, he said," Take it. I have kept some for her." I was startled with some sound and looked out through window lest it should be police out there. I was in a flutter, but Gedu was carefree; intent upon sipping his cup of tea. People like him don't care for police or court. I once again wheedled, "Dear Gedu; who is she? You told me last month; is this the same?"

"Whom I was talking about? I can't recall anything." He countered with a question. Such a question would make even an ascetic throw tantrums. What kind of dogged person he is! Borrowed two thousand rupees from me pleading emergency. Then told that he needed money for treatment of a lady who is distantly related to him, but now dismisses it completely! He always tells in such a way whenever he borrows money. Sometimes his uncle's problem, sometimes another uncle, sometimes the hostel fees of his cousin. He knows that I will never refuse him. I always remain sure that he tells a blatant lie; he will never send money to his uncle or any other relative, but will squander it away all for somebody else. Has mastered the amorous trick of Krishna!

I don't bother him with questions since he pays me back in a few days. Why should I interlope if has the capacity to manage five wives? Getting out of the bathroom, the lady moved past us in to the room, and said humbly," You enjoy yourselves here, I will get myself ready in a while." She smiled as I looked at her from the corners of my eyes. Medium complexion not exactly dark; about six feet, captivating eyes, age cannot be guessed- there is an attraction. I felt a shiver unknown to myself. Seemed as if I have somewhere seen her.... "When will I get my driving licence, boss? I have been appealing you since a year; this is a fun game for you. Get it done please... get it "Gedu tried to coax me.

I looked at him with annoyance. Hell with your licence! My mind is cluttered with the thoughts of that lady with whom you are touring now. I tried to recollect where I had seen her.. So many couples and families have been coming to this astrology-maestro for consultation. But this lady doesn't look like one of them! Is Gedu making a fool of me? He often speaks such things that you cannot believe or disbelieve. He mastered this cunningness since he started as a helper As he whiffed smoke while enjoying the cool zephyr in the mango orchard, he would often narrate things in such a way as if he had just returned after making trip around the world, "The Cavander cigarette is completely original, brought from Ranchi. What to speak about the item at Kolkata.. Oh.. they would drive you mad. An owner at Raipur got so pleased that he offered a whole carton. How much we two can gobble? I have brought the last bottle for you."

We poverty-stricken friends consume with great pleasure all those rare items that Gedu brings when he comes to our village. But the irony is that, a few ungrateful among us, after gobbling everything, gossip at his back, "Gedu will become a famous thief like Charles Shobhraj, I bet. Or else, where does he get so many things from? Besides, he has become so careless about money that he never asks people who have borrowed some money from him to pay it back! He doesn't care if anyone paid back or not! Huh! Became the great donor-Karna!" The lady now came out groomed up. There was no smell of talcum powder or perfume, but she emanated a fragrance as she walked past us, and humbly said, " I may be a bit late to return." She went out all by herself, and Gedu went up to the gate conversing in whispers, and saw her off. They were chatting quite cautiously so that the slightest sound should not flow on to my ears. Gedu asked me as he came back from near the gate, "Will you get me my licence this month?"

Gedu thinks I cannot guess anything. Therefore, he is talking evasively. I wished to thrash the back of that idiot with my fist. Satisfying his anger upon me since I haven't got him his licence? The stupid cannot understand that the brokers do not any more have any influence these days. If we could earn from the RTO office, why would I have become an astrologer? When the brokering business was closed,I had to start a new business. Hung a new name plate on the gate, changed my name too - Pundit Patitapaban Sharma.

Astrology maestro, Utkalratna. Consultation Hour: 10 am to 10pm except Sunday. Guaranteed solution of any problem, be it family matter, social, education, business or politics related. Phone no-0674- 9898989. One always looks for a way when landed in trouble. But, should we ignore our honour, dignity and respectability for that matter! Look at me ! I am earning like a gentleman, getting obeisance from a number of people every day. Gedu does not have a sense of self-respect. He is just a std-8-fail.; how can he have such wisdom?. Much of his words, work, and even dream is meaningless, insensible and absurd.

He moves forward without considering the appropriateness of person, place or time. We were once listening to the radio, which Gedu had brought, reclining in the mango orchard. Few people in our locality possessed radios at that time. He suddenly asked still enjoying the song, "Do you know, whom I have brought this radio for?" I didn't pay him a heed since I was absorbed in a melodious song flowing from Radio Ceylone. He now repeated his question, and made a startling revelation - brought it for Pratima" Leaning against a tree, with eyes closed, I was in a reverie in harmony with the song; but jumped with a start as if scalded by embers, and asked him to clear my doubts, "for whom?"

-"Pratima."

He was thinking of something like a philosopher looking intently towards the river. It seemed to me that the river was there in one of his eyes, and Pratima in the other one. I surveyed him purposefully. He has not of course grown taller an inch in these five years of helpering, but from the way he groomed himself up, and his cheeks that have now become chubby, he looked like the manager of Hari Sahoo's shop.

Pratima is presently not there in the village. How did he get to know her address! She is now studying B. Sc at Cuttack. Staying in the hostel. I am of course pursuing B.A. at Bholanath College, but have updated news about Cuttack. Have already carried Pratima twice this year from the village to the bus stop seating her behind me on my bicycle. She comes to village on holidays. She is no more reserve and silent; quite talkative now. Sitting at my back on the bicycle she would constantly chatter up to the banyan tree; and getting down would walk the rest path. She wanted to be a doctor; but his family didn't support. Now studying B.Sc with a scholarship. All her women-friends are smart; look down upon the ones hailing from rural areas....

She had sprayed on her a perfume of an unfamiliar fragrance. While carrying her on bicycle, a gust of wind often smears that fragrance on my body and it stays on in my shirt for three days turning me exhilarated and oblivious. She told me the other day that boys and girls use to chat for long sitting under the Goldmohur tree in front of her hostel. There is no such restriction as it is there in villages. She has invited me to go to Cuttack. Has told me her room number in the hostel, and the hostel phone number. I haven' t told anything about this to Gedu, why would I ? Am I a fool like him! Gedu perhaps imagines that Pratima will look into his eyes and smile when she gets the radio! Ok. Dear Gedu! Continue with your thought! Yours after all is the wit of a helper, carry on how long you can. Ever seen your face in the mirror? Squatted face like an owl, curly hair, ebony coloured. If your skin was white, people would think you a Nepalese Bahadur. Such a man has planned to gift the radio to Pratima. She would listen to songs, and would think of him while listening to the songs. I smiled in my thought, and asked, "When are you going to join your duty?" I asked him in such a way that as if his answer was insignificant for me. I therefore didn't lend him an ear.

I noticed the next afternoon thad Pratima's younger brother was messing up with the radio, trying to connect to a station. I paused; this is the very same radio!

- "Did you purchase this new radio,Muna?"

- " Oh Yes, Bulu bhai. Please see why it cannot connect to Cuttack Station." I inspected the radio from all its sides. Yes, it is the very same radio. I wished to dash it right there. I was trembling with anger, but could not speak anything.. Tuning to Cuttack Station I gave the radio back, and decided that the letter which, though I had written before a week and was vacillating about whether to post or not, shall on a priority, be posted tomorrow morning even though I might be delayed by an hour to reach college.

It will take not more than a day or two to reach Cuttack. People working in public transport sector are very loose, Gedu says so. Be it driver, helper, owner or even the garage-owner, none of them has a single home or address. They will develop a new relationship wherever their vehicle will run. Once, parking the vehicle on the side of a deserted road, Daulat said, "Dear, do keep a watch - I'll be back in a while." They were on their way back from Paradeep to Keonjhar. The vehicle didn't have the load of goods.

Gedu knew that Daulat would never come back before an hour, and he was the owner of the vehicle till then. So he began to dabble his hand with the steering wheel. He had in the meanwhile learnt driving from Daulat. Fifteen minutes after Daulat was gone, someone knocked the door near the driver's seat, and shouted in a police-style, "Hey, you! Why parked the vehicle here, eh! Your father's land, huh ?" Gedu could see there were four persons in civil dress. There was no chance that Daulat would return soon; and trouble began knocking at the door. " Get down... get down immediately... who gave you permission...."

Two of the tipsy four were shouting. With his sharp presence of mind, Gedu could sense danger if he argued. So he immediately started the vehicle with the plea that he was checking the pressure, and moved on. He knew that there would not be any problem in the next market square. Daulat would instinctively reach the right place. Gedu's job as a helper went on smoothly, but he could not rid himself of the intoxication of Pratima. I was quite watchful of him but dodging my eyes, he gifted Muna a bicycle, T-shirt and perfume.

Even gave money for Muna's form fill-up for matriculation. I got all this news much later. He had thought that I wouldn't be able to know. But I had set my agents to provide me information. Ok, dear Gedu! You continue with your secret dreams; I am stepping along my plans. We used to write letters to each other regularly. She writes very little. Says, theirs is a very rude matron. Switches off the lights at ten in the evening. She cannot therefore write much. Such letters are not after all written in the day. It often gets 12 in the night when I finish writing a letter. She was in B.Sc. and me in B.A.; everything was going on well. But the irony is, her family got her married to a doctor soon after her examination. "It is not easy to make out the game Time plays." Gedu taught me this philosophy when he came to village.

But he never uttered a word about Pratima's marriage. Even thouh he didn't speak anything about it, I could notice fleeting Sannyasi- like symptoms in him. He even told about going on a pilgrimage to Haridwar. But to his misfortune, he lost his job when transport of iron ore was clamped down, the owner of the vehicle could not pay off the loans, and as a result his trucks were seized by the lending bank. After two months of loitering in the Badambadi bus Stand, Gedu began his job as a helper in a bus, and soon became the conductor. Now he completely forgot the matter of Haridwar I could not pass graduation. What should I do there staying in the village?

With recommendation of my uncle I joined BR Pharmaceuticals as a Medicine Representative at Cuttack. After a year's search, I traced Pratima's husband, Dr. Daityari Patnaik, and reached his residence along with office bag in hand. I delightedly introduced me "I hail from the village of your father-in-law, Sir." That hard-hearted doctor didn' t even ask me to sit; he rather sent me back with a caution, " I don't allow MRs to come to my home. You may meet me at my clinic. Don't mind, Please." His behaviour seemed like a slap on my face. Did I join this nomadic job of Medicine . Representative only to earn some money! It hurt me a lot. I resigned from the job the next day, and after a few months, started to learn brokering at the RTO office under the guidance of Parshu bhai. I solaced myself - there is no gain in thinking of the past affairs.

I got married the next year. My wife stayed at village. I go home on Saturdays Gedu did not marry. Who would ever have given him his daughter in marriage? Was anything about him unknown to people? People have seen him carrying so many ladies, when he became the Conductor, seating them beside him that too at no cost. Took them touring; fed them, and many other things. Is there ever a smoke without fire? He used to spend in the company of friends when he was a helper. When he became the Conductor, he earned a lot more, but pretended that nothing of his money was left for saving, if ever anyone asked him for his help. People rumoured that he had kept one at Dhenkanal, another at Baripada, and one more at Bhadrak.

His earnings would not be enough for him; who would think of the village-friends? People even gossip to have seen him carrying girls from Bengal. He never says me anything about all this. I once spent from my purse and made him gulp four pegs with the hope that he might divulge the truth under intoxication. He had finished his four pegs when I was still with the first one. When he was getting inebriated, I seized the opportunity and asked, "Gedu, whom do you gift the sarees, bangles, amul, talcum powder that you purchase? You are no more going to village; whom do you gift all this then?" Seized by intoxication, he opened his eyes, and began to stutter, "Which sarees? Who? Have you ever lost your money I had borrowed? Tell me! All nonsense, self- interested... give me one more peg..." He is able to tell blatant lies even under so much intoxication! When he had gone out to bring betel keeping his bag in my residence just a day before the Savitri festival the last month, I had found these things in the bag when I secretively searched it. But he now disproves all I had seen! He then took the bag with him when he went to his bus at night, but now denies it! "Who is this lady, dear? Tell me the truth. Why hide it from me? Should there be a secret at such an age?"

He was then hunting through the bag. Taking out three photographs, he said, "See the photos,who they are? Can you recognise?" A photo of two women looking like mother and daughter, I could recognise the mother - the lady whom I see today... The girl might be her daughter. Before I could say anything, Gedu told in sombre voice, "She is my daughter." He handed me two more photos and said, "You look at these photos; just give me ten rupees, I'll bring some paan. "Anyone can say that those are photos of the mother and the daughter, taken at different times and places. The mother has embraced the daughter while the daughter has put her arms around her mother's neck. When did Gedu get married? Did he marry at a court without informing us! The girl in the photo seems to be fifteen or sixteen. Did Gedu got this affair done when he was a helper! What a courage of this five-foot sly: eh!

Unable to guess anything, I was just weaving many unrelated things when Gedu and that lady came back. The lady had a bag full of vegetable in one hand and a broomstick in the other. Whispering between themselves near the gate perhaps about some unresolved matter, they entered my house. I was observing everything through the window - Gedu was only nodding to all he listened. Their interaction, activity and relationship seemed rather mysterious. Gedu asked me when he saw the photo in my hand, "Did you recognise my daughter? You have never seen her. See her photo sincerely quot; The lady now said, "I have bought some vegetable at the market square. Going to cook something. The house is rather untidy; this is quite usual if there is not a woman at home." With these words she went into the kitchen as she got the broomstick ready.

Unable to wait anymore, I pulled Gedu on to the sofa, and asked, "O Guru, first tell me when you got married? Is she your..." Before I could complete my question, he shouted, "Laxmi! Come here. The Pundit wants you here." And asked me with a smile, "Can't you recognise Laxmi?" I was in a great trouble. Should I say yes or no? I only looked away stupidly. Laxmi said as she noticed the photos in my hand, "She is Pratima's daughter. Stays with me at Baripada." Pratima's daughter!

But Gedu says she is his daughter! I could feel a drum beating inside my head, it could burst any moment! Pratima-daughter - Gedu- Laxmi - I was runable to make out the crux. Fifteen or twenty years have of course passed in the mean time. Who after all has kept information about others? Where is the time to think about others when one's own problems seem insurmountable. Not that I sat completely silent after I had returned that the day from the doctor, pocketing the insult. I would many times go past his residence, buy bread from the shop in front of his residence; look eagerly at the closed door, and the doorbell; but could never muster courage to climb the steps.

Gedu was intently searching something from inside his bag. With his eyes still fixed inside the bag he said. "Did you recognise Laxmi or not? Pratima's maternal cousin; often visited our village. Haven't you seen her?"

"Did you show to brother all your records or not?"

Laxmi asked Gedu emphatically, and then told me,

"Brother, you haven't yet stepped in our house. Please, do sometime visit Baripada. We are of course poor, but our heart is not small. Tilu bhai comes, every month' his bus is now plying. You please visit some time. Ever been to Similipal? quot;

"Where is Pratima now? At Baripada?" I asked unable to hold back my suspicion. I did not have the least interest about the residence of these people; I was curious about the depth of the relationship between Gedu and Pratima.

Laxmi suddenly turned pale with my question. A manifest despondency enveloped her being as if someone thrust upon her tons of sorrow. Eyes brimming with tears, she looked as if weeping. Swallowing the saliva, she asked me innocently. "Don't you really know anything about her?" I became unusually worried; and apprehensive, too. I Kept looking at Laxmi's quivering lips in fear and apprehension. "Pratima has been staying at Koraput since ten years. Now a teacher at Nandapur Aashram School. The poor girl! None of us ever imagined that such a misfortune would befall her." Laxmi wiped tears with the sleeve of her saree.

"Where is the doctor saab now? Transferred to koraput? He had perhaps been to America, for a research! " I asked desperately. And thought that, it was necessary for that hard-hearted doctor to be transferred to Koraput. Become a doctor means you won't care anyone! Won't have regards for anyone!

People will seem to you as patients or else insects! I had kept track of him until a year after I had left my job as an M.R. He used to visit Aarogya Clinic. Employees of the clinic told that the doctor had been to America. That much. I don't have any more information about him!! "That is a fraud," Laxmi shouted in anger as I mentioned about the doctor. Had got a job with forged certificate. We could not get an wink about it. They had come with marriage proposal. His father then told that they didn't need anything in dowry, but only a bride.

Or else, could Pratima's family ever think of getting a doctor as their son-in-law? Therefore they agreed. But the matter of forged certificate was revealed after five years. That thief is now in jail. "Oh my God!" I beat my hands on head. Such a cheating!

"What then?"

"A mountain collapsed on Pratima. " Heaving sighs, Laxmi wiped her nose as she was sobbing. I kept looking away already turned speechless.

"Pratima's in-laws then threw her out of their home. Her daughter was only two years old. Already dying of shame, she didn't wish to return to her parents. Stayed with me for three years until she got a job. Her daughter and my son are of the same age; they studied together in the same class. We are not a well-to-do family; survive on the meager income from the vegetable shop of my husband. Tilu bhai has been bearing all her expenses; could we otherwise give her education?"

I didn't have courage or strength to believe all that I was listening. So many incidents passed, but I could not know anything! What could after all I do even if I knew! But, this Gedu! How did he got all the news?

"Where is the girl studying now?"

"Pursuing intermediate, staying in a hostel in Bhubaneswar. I had now gone to meet her. She hasn't been home for four months; exams in the next month. I gave her the mess charges, and the exams, fees."

She looked at Gedu with eyes of gratitude.

Gedu was listening everything dispassionately as if there was nothing new about all this. Like a vehicle traversing roads full of ascents and descents, these incidents have passed away before him. "You must often be meeting Pratima. Where did you meet her after her marriage, Gedu?" My question was not at all unexpected for Gedu. He perhaps expected that I would ask him such a question. He expressed reluctance, and looking evasively up at the ceiling, tried to recollect. "I had been to Baripada with my bus, fifteen years back. I met her there in the bus. I didn't have any idea about her family. I was on the conductor's seat; she was at the window on the opposite side along with her little daughter. She smiled a little when her eyes fell on me, and then tried to make her child sleep. The child was obstinately crying all the while enquiring, "Where's papa where's papa..." Passengers had already got annoyed as they could not sleep because of the child's crying. The child didn't stop crying despite all her mother's attempts. Finding no other way, I asked Pratima to give the child to me; let me try out.

Surprisingly, the child stopped crying just as she sat on my lap. Played with my pen, receipt book and handbag; fiddled with my beard and moustache and scratched, and after a while, fell asleep on mybosom right upto Baripada. Pratima wanted to take her after she was asleep, but I refused. The little girl tied me from that very moment, with a bond, an intimacy that I felt as if my own daughter had slept on my bosom; let her continue to sleep there. Then I heard everything from Laxmi. The few words I had then exchanged with Pratima in the bus was it all ;

nothing more. Honestly speaking, I didn't have the patience to look at her weeping face."

"Don't you ever take your bus to Koraput?" I asked suspiciously.

" No, why should I?" I could feel a heaviness in his voice. He perhaps felt insulted with my question. He continued, leaving a long sigh, "I talk with Laxmi, meet her. I am bound to meet her or else, who will take care of my daughter? Her studies? Who will make her a doctor? Conduct her marriage? What do you think! An uneducated, drunkard, helper, conductor, not married and became a father - Can't he discharge the duties of a father?"

Gedu suddenly turned silent, as if he was determined to accomplish an iron resolve to the letter. That determination and firmness was clearly manifest in his face. Even though teardrops gathered in the corners of his eyes, he cautiously tried to keep them hidden from me just as he had kept the story of his daughter hidden from me for fifteen years. "Leave all this. I haven't yet told you the main thing for which Laxmi has forcibly brought me here. You first of all listen to that matter." He now tried to laugh out. "Which matter, anymore?" I looked at him stupidly. Laxmi has brought me here to consult a good doctor. I don't believe these doctors. I told her that my friend is a great astrologer-pundit; I'll obey his advice. You just calculate and tell me how long I am now going to live. Will I survive or not till my daughter completes her study, even though I may not till her marriage? Don't people ever survive with stomach ailments? Take, and go through these papers." He handled to me a bunch of prescriptions, medicine bills, reports of endoscopy and ultrasound and others, and crouched on the sofa as if just relieved off all tension.

Slum

A police van! So early in the morning! It is not at all a new or surprising thing that the police should come to this criminal slum. Raids are quite often carried out here. The Intelligence report reveals that this place is a den of thieves, antisocial and hardcore criminals. Antisocial elements chalk out their plans of action here. It is wise to erase the germinating ground of criminals. Therefore the raids are. But there is not one or two policemen today.. ; rather a complete procession of police personnel. All geared up with rifle, baton, shield and helmet. An intensive raid is going to be carried out, it seems. May be, some terrorist has hidden here! Some drug peddler or a criminal from a neighbouring state may have slipped in to this place considering it a safe haven ! The criminals may have thought that even the stray dogs or cattle, even though routed, wouldn't come to this place, let alone the police.

The T.V. reporters have also come today as if they had been waiting with a sleepless night to come here in the morning. The matter must then be an important one. Well the matter will become clear after a few minutes of waiting. About half the population of the slum had got up early in the morning, as they are wont to. Mitu Puhan had been hurrying to take and queue up his auto-rickshaw in the stand, and wait for the Howrah-Puri passenger train which is about to arrive in a short while. When he was about to worship his auto- rickshaw after he had cleaned it, a police officer called him.

- "Hey, man! Do you stay here? What is your name?"

- "Mitu Puhan, Sir."

- "How long have you been staying?"

-"About three years, Sir.

"Do you know these three?" The police officer held before him a

piece of paper that had the names of three people written on it. And, ordered in a slightly harsh voice," move with us, and identify these three criminals."

A constable who had in the meanwhile held Mitu's hand gave him a light push just as the officer concluded his words, and said "move on." Mitu was surprised to see the list of the criminals because he had never known anything about their crime. He guessed that the police might look for Tula or Kala. He knew about their arrest in the matter of necklace snatching, and apprehended that they might have been involved in some other unlawful activity. Or at least, the police could have looked for Padia Rout who was involved in a brawl at the autorickshaw stand. A year ago, when Padia was bargaining the fare with a couple of passengers, another driver came forward to ride those passengers for a less fare. There began the wrangle. Since the other driver was a local guy, he took the matter up to the police. If it is not Tuna or Padia, the police should definitely look for Babula as he had been accused of beating the police for which he had to spend a night at the police station. He was such a naive who didn't know how to speak with the different types of people. He sells Golgappa at the market square.

People crowd up near him in the evening. The other day, two guys ate Golgappa of twenty-two rupees, and were trying to flee away saying that their uncle would pay the money as they pointed fingers at a policeman standing nearby. Babula wouldn't relent, he grabbed one of them, dragged him to the police, but let him go when the police said that the guy was his boy. The matter would not have gone any further; but when the crowd thinned away after an hour, Babula asked the police uncle for money, "Twenty-five rupees, sir."

The uncle stared at him harshly, but Babula was still unable to decipher the meaning of that look. "The guys have eaten of thirty rupees, Sir, But would I take thirty rupees from you?" Babula said politely. The uncle could not control his anger, and fumed," Where do you prepare all this, eh? Making it at unhygienic and dirty places, and spreading disease, you all idiots!" Babula couldn't still understand, and begged, "Twenty rupees will do, sir. " "Want money? Ok! Come to the police station," the uncle dragged Babula to the police station. There are four or five more people who have at some time or the other spent night at the police station, but none of their name is there in the list! Mitu Puhana could not crack the mystery. He only had been moving ahead, with light pushes at his back, towards the house of these criminals.

The matter will become clear if we learn the history of this criminals' slum before trying to identify the criminals. The place didn't have its name as Criminals' Slum from the beginning. When a number of people from different corners of the state gathered here, all in search of some job, and began to settle here, someone called the place as Laborers' Slum. Initially, about twenty or twenty-five laborers settled here followed by masons, carpenters, autorickshaw drivers and a variety of unskilled labourers. Government land; making the roof with a few asbestos sheets, plastering the inner wall and hanging a door was enough to make a house. Canal water was available nearby; so there was no need to worry about water.

After the tension of staying in a house was over, the tension of finding work also vanished. The B.T.A. Company started construction of 300 houses under the Rose Valley Dream Home Project. The company had been successfully carrying out its projects in different cities of the country for affluent beneficiaries. Good luck smiled on the Labourer's Slum as the labourers didn't have to go too far to find a job. Now, they had at their hand work for five years.

The place had its name as Laboure's Slum for five years. When the Dream Home Project came to its close, some house-owners came to live there, and some others rented their houses as they had their residence elsewhere in the city. The residents of the project then guessed that whatever minor thefts were done in their houses were actually committed by people of this slum. There was after all, no other habitation nearby. And, only gentlefolk lived in the Rose Valley who never steal from others' houses. So, thieves are coming from this Laborer's Slum. It is in this context that a house-owner of the Rose Valley suggested to his friends a name for this slum, which sounded somewhat logical - Crimanls' Slum. Thereafter, the identity of Labourers' slum changed to "Criminals' Slum."

The babu's of Rose valley never come to the Criminals' Slum; the people of the slum rather go to work in their houses. All the people who cleaned utensils, in the houses of the babus, swept floor, drove their cars, cleaned weed from their lawn, took their dogs for morning chores or cleaned their toilet tanks lived here in this slum. The Rose Valley was getting radiant with new colours. Like the strips of colourful light brightening the fountain of water, the dazzle and attraction of the babus-memsaabs, their children, and even their pet animal was also attaining new dimension. Buses of most expensive schools had started plying up to their houses. Best doctors of the city had already set up clinics at the Valley. Food, drinks, roads or entertainment- everything was lavishly available to the residents of the valley. It seemed as if all the blessings of God was getting showered upon them. But the picture of the Criminals Slum situated just 200 meters away was completely different. The name of the slum changed, but never its picture.

One speciality of this slum was that scarcity never left its people. How so much they toiled and earned, they all had the same situation of wanting. Hawker, tailor, plumber, mason, contract labourer, coolie, trolley rickshaw puller or driver - whatever type of people lived here, they all had a common symptom - wanting. Unhygienic environment, stinking smell, dirty water flowing through the roads, scarcity of drinking water, and very little electric light. - Two hundred families lived here along with their hens, ducks, dogs, parrots, pet rats, trolley rickshaws, auto rickshaws, religious activities, asthmatic parents, and girls who are past their school-going age. All the curse of God had flooded the slum, it seemed. The existence of Criminals Slum always suffocated the residents of Rose vallly like a wound on the forehead of a healthy body.

Now let's identify the criminals. Mitu knows them all, but is surprised to see their names in the list as he is not aware how dangerous they have been recorded to be in the police file. The first criminal is Kalakar Mohapatra alias Kalu Mohapatra. He has been charged with the sections 420 and 308. Serious charges of cheating, swindling and attempt to murder have been levelled against him. Kalu has been working as a mason since the beginning of the Rose valley Project. After a few days of working as a mason, he switched to become a labourer-contractor. Started to provide masons and labourers for the construction of buildings at a rate of 50 rupees per sqft. The owner would provide bricks, stone, chips, sand and cement, and Kalu provided the workers. The owners wanted quick completion of their houses, for which Kalu hired more workers from the nearby villages. Workers also preferred to work with Kalu as he cleared their wage every week, and often helped them with their food and accommodation.

Adequate job was not available in villages; and whatever little job was there, the wages were even less. When the daily wage in the villages was Rs. 30/- it was Rs. 150/- in the city. Kalu managed his work with the help of 3 teams. Since he was able to complete a project even before the scheduled time, he had earned some respect from the house-owners. Everything was going well until once a house owner alleged that Kalu had been stealing his cement. He had perhaps gathered evidence. The owner was quite shrewd, and cautious. Taking advantage of the alliance he had with a contractor engaged in constrution of a bridge over the Mahanadi river, he often tactfully brought 100 or 200 cements from him for half the price. There was no chance that Kalu or his workers could know the matter. Why should they bother as to where the owner was procuring the cement, chips or the iron bars from? But when the owner went to visit the under- construction house of his friend at the other end of the city, he noticed there the very same cement packets . He alone knows where Horse-brand cement is available; it is not available in the market. So, he didn't have any doubt about it. He came back and charged Kalu straight away.

How so much Kalu swore and pleaded, the owner didn't relent. After a calculation, he reported that cements worth 1.5 lakh have been swindled from the beginning, and the amount would be adjusted from Kalu's bill. The matter was not completely true or untrue. The labourers often took intoxicants in order to relax from their physical strain. They used to work overtime so that they could send more money to their home. It required more physical strain, but there should be enough energy in the body. Some workers smoke ganja to forget the mental and physical pain. They didn't always have money with them as they got their wage at the end of a week. As a result, a packet of cement or two disappear every month. The owner had piled a hill of cements.

If one or two packets are taken away, it would be like taking away a palmful of water from the ocean. Everybody was surprised to hear about embezzlement of Rs 1.5 lakh. Kalu argued that if cement worth 1.5 lakh was taken away, could the building be constructed only with sand and chips? How could the pillars be fixed? But the owner wouldn't listen. He was sure that no one else would be able to reach that man through whom he could reach the Horse- brand cement. Evidently, the cement he discovered at the construction site of his friend's house has been sourced from here. When the argument rose up to a hustle, the owner jostled Kalu roughly. Kalu was not to give in; he gave the owner such a violent thrust at his nape that the poor men fell to the ground on a heap of centering material. A shred of the material pierced his left palm. That's all. And then, Kalu became a criminal. The owner framed against him the charges of attempt to murder, cheating, swindling, violation of agreement, and a couple more. After a sentence of three months of jail, Kalu was freed on a bail.

The second warrantee on the list of the police is Tuna Behera alias Parthasarathi Behera. He is an electric mechanic. There was government case against him. Staying since long in Criminals' Slum. A native of Nilagiri, he has his parents and siblings settled in village. He is the eldest son; now 35 but still not married. When their crops was totally destroyed by elephants, he came here to the capital city in search of job. There was no other way; the four members of his family had looked up to his earnings. Tuna is only a matriculate, but with a sharp presence of mind. Had learnt some electrical skill only by observing. He always keenly observed when an uncle of his did sundry electrical work at the village. Often enquires, and helps him. Simply with a guess, he could correctly diagnose why a fan is running slow, or why there is a voltage discrepancy in different rooms of the house. He came forward to the city with the lone treasure of that much knowledge, and a huge confidence; and turned a complete electrician.

He engaged a guy pursuing ITI course in his work; and starting off with minor wiring work, he took up the entire electrical work of buildings. Employed two assistants on monthly salary basis. There was a special work that Tuna alone was able to do, and no other electrician even dared to attempt that. He could bypass the electric metre. And as a result, how so much energy one may consume, the meter would never show that much reading. Since Tuna alone was able to do this intricate work, he was in a great demand. The owners who had installed heaters and ACs at home badly needed Tuna. The electricity bill which ordinarily comes about Rs 500/- would soar up to about Rs 3000/- when heaters and run. The owners look up to Tuna as they are aware of such calculation. Each of the elegant palaces that adorn the Rose Valley Have multiple ACs, geysers and heaters installed in them. Can one ever live without such articles ? How would they live with so much heat in summer and so much cold in winter? Therefore, they need and deal with tuna with great affection. And Tuna earns quite handsomely from such work. 2000/-for the initial bypassing; and 100/- for bimonthly checking and maintenance. He goes all by himself to carry out such work. The babus offer him tea and snacks, and talk with him quite fondly.

A phone call once came from one of the babus of the Rose Valley. Tuna had already previously worked at his house. The babu was perhaps an SDO or a higher officer working in the Electricity department. He shouted as he saw Tuna. "How come the bill of 4000/- this time? It used to be about seven or eight hundred every month. What the hell this time? I paid you your fees, but you didn't do your work properly. I'll now pay 4000/- because of your mistake?

"The babu fumed in anger." I am looking into it, Sir. Perhaps, it has become direct." Tuna gently replied as though a criminal he was. "What will you look into, eh?" the babu countered in a fury. "Here is the bill in my hand. It is so much because of your negligence. It is your fault. You have to pay me 4000/- right now. I'll pay the bill; today is the last date for payment!!" Four thousand! and Tuna! He was only pleading. Such mistakes wouldn't repeat, Sir I will fix it."

Officials of the electricity department raided Tuna's house that night. With the rice-cooking utensil on the heater, Tuna had been cutting vegetable to cook curry. The officials seized the heater, some coil, and other electrical equipment. The case that the electricity department had filed with charges of theft of electricity, illegal connection, and use of heater with meter tampering continued for three years. He even had been jailed for fifteen days.

The third criminal was Ashutosh Mahananda alias Ashu

Nanda. Very severe charges have been framed against him: taking laws into his hand, provoking people to damage government property, and encroaching government land. He is sent to jail every year; and is freed in fifteen days. Ashu Nanda has no one of his own. He alone knows what his job is. He has studied a little, but has quite a command over legal matters. Few people of the slum knew him as he was not a native of this locality. He came here lately to stay on rent. The day he assembled the residents of the slum at the roadside-meeting, and standing on the pandal he had built, along with a mike in hand he shouted - Give us, our basic rights.... he became well-known.

Mahananda has stayed in this city for ten years. He has seen the changing scenario of the city - how the highways are getting wider, smooth and beautiful. Construction of ten parks in the city, the artificial fountains dazzling with the bright electric lights, spreading up of tiles every month on foot paths, the gardener carefully trimming the trees as though combing the hair on the medians of roads, and, those who used to gaze an airplane with their heads turned upward are now flying every month. He has seen how the tempo of transformation and progress is moving ahead in a quick pace.

The MLA saheb had sheltered him in his quarters to do sundry work. An orphan, he had been loitering in the village, and shouting slogans for politicians at the time of election. After winning the MLA saheb mercifully brought the chap with him. When he came here, he would fumble while talking with people; and move shyly with his head down. The people who talked to him disrespectfully, like "Hey chap, just see if the saheb is home," had to change their way in five years -" Mahananda Sir, would you please tell Saheb about us?"

But alas! Unable to get the MLA ticket on charges of

anti-party activities, the saheb contested as an independent candidate and lost the trust. Mahananda once again became orphan, and after moving here and there finally stayed in Criminals' Slum on rent.

Mahananda addressed the slum dwellers from the pandal; reminded them of their inherent power, the fundamental rights that the constitution has guaranteed them; and all that they deserved. In fact, the slum dwellers had never found time even to think about this matter. About two hundred families lived in the slum. Three rows of houses, congested like the pigeon's coop. Streams of dirty sewage water flowing through the approach roads. And, the roads are nothing more than the empty spaces between the rows of house. No one has built it; it has automatically been created when houses were built on either side in rows. They are so narrow that it is difficult even for a bicycle to pass if an autorickshaw comes from the other side. The gentlemen living in the heart of the city never tread this place, but Prabhu Prasad Agrawal has in the meanwhile thrice toured the slum. And, the matter has not gone unnoticed by Mahananda. He has learnt the trick of counting feathers even of a flying bird since the time he stayed in the MLA Colony. He knew Agrawal very well. The Marwari always purchased only small-sized incense sticks. If there is no profit, he won't even look at you, let alone smile. Why should he step inside this uncouth slum? Without any interest! Mahananda could not digest the matter.

After an investigation, he came to know that Agrawal has recently purchased 'The King' hotel. He is now trying to upgrade the non- star hotel to a star one for which he has already sent a proposal to the government. Many more 5-star hotels are necessary if the city is to be made world-class. The king hotel would help the government in this mission. But it can be smoothly accomplished if four acres of government land lying adjacent to the hotel is provided on lease for the development of its infrastructure. Prabhu has already applied for the lease, and discussed the matter in several offices and with the minister. But the problem is that the government land Prabhu requires has on it cropped up the Criminals' Slum alias Labourers' Slum. The slum dwellers got scared when Mahananda revealed Agrawal's plan in the meeting. A few agitated people shouted for the demolition of 'The King' hotel, and even hurled stones that broke a couple of window panes. The Criminals' slum Protection Committee was formed amidst such a scary situation; and Ashutosh Mahananda, Kalakar Mohapata and Parthasarathi Behera were declared as its President, vice-President and Secretary respectively. Besides, the 'Long live Ashu Bhai' slogans also reverberated in the meeting place.

The significance of slogans is that wherever they may be shouted, they would definitely resonate in the capital. When 200 voters shouted slogans in favour of Ashutosh, the local politicians and the mayor were terrified. The politicians and government officials invited the Protection Committee for a discussion, before the matter could go out of their control. As a result, a water-tap and a halogen light were installed within a week at one end of the slum. The slum dwellers with were so much happy that they forgot about the Protection Committee.

And exactly after three months, there is a procession of police today, and a celerity to nab the criminals. Three platoon police, Magistrate, loud speaker and TV reporters. Must be a very serious plan. The police officer explained the matter to the magistrate- It is an order from the top, Sir. The operation has to be completed by 12 noon. There will be no problem if these three miscreants are taken away. They have been provoking and misguiding the slum dwellers. The recently framed law states that we can evict without prior notice. There is no problem, Sir. Two bulldozers will reach here in just five minutes. More force, if needed, will be asked for; but we have first of all to nab those three criminals.

Prabhu Prasad had kept a vigilant look on the situation from behind the window of 'The King' hotel while praying God with a ghee-filled lamp. "Oh Lord ! May today's operation become successful with

your blessings!"

Race Course

Aditya Babu startled up as he looked at the wall clock. It's ten past nine in the morning. Already ten minutes late! Getting defeated after a phase of intense war, he would by now have ended up becoming a horse. Elephant, bear, the monkey playing cymbals, giraffe, five teddies - all are ready; but where is the real warrior? She should not have been late! He shouted with worry and concern, "Khusi! You are late!"

Aditya Babu is always in his wonted habit, since his student days, to arrive or begin his work exactly on time. Even the peon with the duty to ring the bell feels ashamed when he sees Aditya Babu ready, with the students' attendance register, chalk and duster at the door of the staff room, to visit his class but he himself is late by two minutes to ring the bell. It has been ten years since he retired from his job. His sense of punctuality has not slackened a bit despite his advancing age, household pressures or casual ailments. To leave the bed early morning at five, make tea after getting done his morning activities, serve his wife with tea after waking her up from sleep, go out on morning walk, and bring fresh vegetable from the market while coming back - all these activities go on like the moving of hands of the wall clock. The rendezvous at the Walker's Club gets quite intimate. Laughing boisterously with togetherness, sometimes silent prayer, ruminations, and sometimes endearing talk goes on everyday there among the fifteen -twenty of the members of the club. Aditya babu has been active there for the last ten or twelve years.

"Shall I bring you tea?" Usha Devi brought Aditya Babu back to consciousness as she shook him by his shoulders. "What have you been looking at those elephants and horses for? Are you day by day turning a child. You have already turned seventy! I have ordered idli for your breakfast -I will be fasting as it is Sankranti today."

Aditya Babu looked with contentment at Usha Devi from the corners of his eyes, and spread a smile on his lips. "What more is left unattained that still more fasting; and Sankranti! Is it advance booking for the next birth?"

"Huh, I don't like such mocking words of yours." Usha Devi looked ruddy with feigned anger, and said as she moved a little away- "Bunu telephoned last night. I didn"t wake you up as you were snoring in deep sleep. Told, he wouldn't be able to come the month as his application for leave has been rejected. His company is not in a good position now - he is sad about it." Usha Devi's face looked pale and overcast as she concluded the report. All luster faded away, she sat quiet and downcast. Adity babu could read the eyes of his wife, and the somber face of his wife. They have now lived their conjugal life for forty years. Even though one doesn't open up the lips, many untold tales of the heart become clearly read and understood. Bunu is their only child whose success story used to be cited by many parents as examples for their own children. They would advise them to look up to Bunu as an ideal- "You should study like the son of Aditya Mohapatra; see, how his photograph has come up in the newspaper. Blessed are his parents.

What a talented child! Yet to complete the studies, but an American company has offered him a salary of one lakh dollar! You know how much money one lakh dollar means!" Soon after his completion of MTech from IIT Delhi, the IBM company offered him a job at Texas with an annual salary of one lakn dollar. He was quite industrious and punctual, exactly like his father.

By the sheer dint of hard labour and experience, he has been climbing stairs of success in just ten years. After changing three companies, he is presently the CEO of Blitz Software company in Canada. After marrying his Bengali classmate, he now settles in Toronto. The grandson is going to turn three in a few days, but Usha Devi could not yet fondle him in her lap. She was excited that they were coming, but she is now full of tears when she learnt that they won't be coming. "As we grow up, our expectations change, and attitude too. All that seem invaluable and attractive during youthful days turn valueless in old age. But the little wishes, even though they may not have any monetary values, when fulfilled saturate the heart with immense joy." Aditya Babu has many times told this truth to Usha Devi. There was a time when he used to boast with great delight the success story of his son. He had not, of course, developed at that time diabetes or blood pressure nor did Usha Devi have problem with the knees or use waist corset. Now, they have to consult the doctor in every little matter of their living. Usha Devi swells up with anger if ever Aditya Babu grabs a sweetmeat out of greed.

Aditya babu has become extremely worried. The game could not yet start. Khusi always came running even with a single call; but even after calling out for her twice today, she is not coming, nor is there her response with words" yes, grandpa... I'm coming...!" Did she become so lazy ! Khusi has not been able to speak clearly. She mumbles a lot but if Aditya Babu cannot get to hear her ramblings in the morning, the whole day seems sour to him. He woud often say, "Khusi is my real medicine and tonic."

When Aditya babu was ill a year ago, he didn't like to talk with anyone. Everybody seemed to him an enemy. Nights passed by sleep less, he didn't savour any food; no medicine worked on him. After a thorough examination, Dr. B D Palei diagnosed it was depression. And the cause was excessive mental stress over a certain matter. Khusi at that time was just beginning to move on her knees. When she crawled and smiled at Aditya babu with her toothless mouth, his depression gradually began to evaporate. When she started walking and messed with the table and scattered books from the shelves, Aditya babu's depression completely vanished; he regained agilityand smartness.

Even though Usha Devi didn't greatly appreciate such childish delight of her husband, she didn't oppose him either. Even though smiles bloomed on her lips with a glance of Khusi, she could notsoak her heart with joy. Khusi, afterall, was not her own granddaughter! So much intimacy with the tenant is never good!

Aditya babu startled with the word 'tenant.' He never expected such a word from Usha Devi. Had Prabhanjan and Urmila not been there that day, where would be Usha now? It was only six months ago. When she was about to offer worship in the morning, she whirled and fell down hard on the verendah. She had high blood pressure for which she used to take medicine regularly. Aditya babu had not by the time come back from his morning walk. Who carried her to hospital at such a crucial moment without the slightert delay? Who nursed her then with great care for fifteen days ? Anyone other than this couple? Should one grossly call such people tenants simply because they are staying on rent? There was a vacillating situation. It seemed to Aditya babu that all this power, position, property, fame or public honour was not at all necessary. And what he truly needs- Bunu is not able to understand.

It is of course quite natural on his part not to be able to understand if his position, age and the place he is in are considered. But after witnessing Niranjan babu's situation, it is difficult for a father, let alone

Aditya babu, to keep patience. Niranjan babu's family means his wife Ratnagarbha, and the three sons - one outshining the other. The first two sons-doctors- now settled in Australia. The youngest one-a professor, now works at Johannesberg University. After the death of his wife, Niranjan babu's only job now is to keep looking at the vacant street from his balcony.

He is completely dependent on his maid servant for everything- his morning tea, breakfast, lunch, dinner, blood pressure tablets, even for a glass of water. If any day the maid falls ill, Niranjan babu has to observe a fast that day. An active member of the Walkers' Club, he reveals his heart to Aditya babu considering him very close. Often visits him only to have a cup of tea made by Usha Devi. It seems when you look at him that he of course has life, but there is no lustre in it, not even the slightest stirring. He wishes he would gather joy in this fag end of his life by ruminating the memories of his bygone days. Everyone should seek his advice as the head of the family before beginning anything, even though it may be for a short while only. He would buy toys for his grandchildren, play with them, quarrel with them, and would show them birds seating them on his shoulder.

Getting his eyes checked, his son would change the hazy spectacles-

- He has nestled in his heart so many of such hopes and dreams. He would often ask out of habit a boy passing by, "What is your name, O child? Your father's name?" The boy would laugh aloud and reply.

"Didn't ask me yesterday? Forget , eh"

Alas! Niranjan babu's nights were too short lived for so many dreams. He passed away two months ago with heart attack. Obsequies were performed with the help of neighbours and the eldest son arrived after fifteen days. He generously thanked the neighbours and expressed his gratitude for them. Requested Aditya Uncle to find a tenant when he gave him the housekeys, and shared with him his bank account number. While carrying away the funeral ashes of his father, he was filled with tears, and he announced in a voice choked with emotion that he would consign some of the ashes in the Bay of Bengal, some in Indian Ocean, and some in the Pacific Ocean to ensure the heavenward journey of his father's soul. Aditya babu has witnessed all this, and has clearly realized how the friendship and support of poor neighbours is much more valuable than top- positioned, millionaire, expat son and daughter-in-law.

Usha Devi does not disclose a lot of things to Aditya babu. Her husband is not aware that she talks with her son and daughter-in-law thrice a week. After Aditya babu falls asleep, she talks with them on phone, even on video call. She can get glimpses of her son, daughter-in-law and grandson only on holidays but on other days it is only Bunu who talks with her. She would always ask the same question,

"What did you eat today? Why do you look so weak?"

And Bunu's reply is "Maa, I have put on two kilos of weight;

have to exercise daily for an hour."

-"Is sprout available there?"

-"Yes, Maa. Everything. Everything is available here except a

father and a mother."

Usha Devi turns somber with such a reply. She silently looks at the screen of the mobile phone; Bunu shows his office chamber, tea- coffee-soup making machine, his colleagues busy with their laptop, and the view of the city from their seventy-second floor. -"Show me your tiffin!"

Bunu would smile at the naiveness of his mother. How would she know what type of food is available in the canteen of a renowned multinational company? He would explain, "Maa! Indian, Chinese, continental-everything is available in our canteen."

-"But, wouldn't that food make you ill? Why, what does Runi do? Can't she prepare tiffin for you? Ask her to talk with me." Usha Devi sends a command to her daughter-in-law. Such commands are issued everytime, but Runi's reply is never received. Usha Devi perhaps forgets that Runi at that time remains busy with her laptop in some other office, talking with a client. The chatting between the mother and the son often leads to argument. The mother asks, "When are you coming? Three years have already passed with your words of 'this month... next month.'

You are cheating me?"

Bunu would console his mother, "Why don't you both come here?

Papa has already retired; why do you stay clinging to that dirty place? Do you think that we can avail leave here just like in Papa's job? No leave is here, only work and work; work in the office or from home."

Bunu would show Lubun, to his mother, through video call on Sundays. Unable to understand anything, the poor child would only stare; and would smile and wave hands with Bunu's instruction. A roly-poly baby, glittering eyes like those of a doll, chubby cheeks, nose and lips resembling his father's. Usha Devi wishes she would gather the child that very moment in her lap, and embrace him in her bosom. Would walk matching with his footsteps while clutching the fingers of that little devil, and would feign anger when he would pee on her... But nothing of that sort ever happens; Usha Devi's eyes rather become moist with a glimpse of the child. She wipes her eyes, hiding it from Bunu. At such times, Runi keeps herself engaged in Kitchen or drawing room.

Finding opportune moments, Bunu arranges for the mother-in- law and the daughter-in-law to see and talk with each other. The mother in-law never forgets to issue her certain instructions, even during that brief conversation, "Do not make the curry oily or spicy; it would upset Bunu's stomach. Why don't you put a dot of collyrium on the forehead of the child? I had reminded you- why don't you put on lac bangles on the wrist?"

Usha Devi knows that her mother-in-law-like admonition will have no impact, still she repeats the same thing every time; and sobs for an hour covering her face in the sleeve of her saree. Bunu doesn't tell anything directly to Aditya babu. Whatever he wants, he tells if through his mother. Could not get rid of the habit even today. Has been insisting upon his mother for a couple of days - persuade Papa to remove the tenants. He also reiterated the same thing last night, but Usha Devi has not yet told anything about this proposal to her husband. She has been waiting for a suitable time.

Or else, all good may turn into bad with a rigid person that Aditya

babu is. The TV mechanic Prabhanjan, his wife Urmila and their little daughter Khusi have been staying with a nominal rent at one side of the house. It is not Bunu's obstinate demand to remove this family from their house, it is rather the result of the calculation of his MBA- educated wife. It is a property of 3500 sqft. area, only 200 metres awary from the 100 ft wide road, and only 1km away from the Omfed Square. The present market price would be about 1.5 crore. The amount, if deposited in a bank, would get an interest of 10 lakhs per annum. But what do they get from it now? The house apart, a hundred or something. coconuts from the two coconut trees, a drumstic tree and a jackfruit tree. Sale of coconut, drumstic or jackfruit is banned; only gift and donation.

The daughter- in-law has planned it well; first, the tenants will be removed. Then the old couple will go to their village for only eight months. The property will be handed over to a builder. He will demolish the old building and construct an apartment; and bear all the expenses. He will hand over five flats out of the total ten flats to the landowner; each one costing one crore. The plan is all ready; the builder is also ready, the old couple will stay in one flat; and people are ready too to buy the rest four flats for four crores.

All that needs to be done is signing agreement with the builder, for which Runi's builder-brother is eagerly ready. But the problem is that the property which Aditya babu had purchased twenty-five years ago with an arrear and a ten-year tenure bank-loan is in his name.

"Bunu had telephoned last night," Usha Devi started the conversation taking advantage of an opportune moment, and handed the cup of tea smilingly to her husband. Aditya babu had fixed his gaze on an obituary published in the newspaper, and was minutely observing the photograph of the deceased as he seemed well-known to him. He therefore did not pay heed to Usha Devi's words or the cup of tea.

"Did Bunu talk with you?" Usha Devi added one more question, but Aditya babu was silent. His gaze was still intent on the photograph of the person who has left for the heavenly abode after spending seventy years here upon this earth. Today is the eleventh day of his obsequious ritual.

"He said he was in a great tension." Fitfully crumpling the newspaper, and throwing it on the teapoy, Aditya babu asked, "yes, tell me, what happened?"

"Bunu said that he was in a great tension ... our neighbours have informed him something over phone."

"Listen, I am also in great tension. Where is Khusi? Just go and find why she did not show up yet!!!." Usha Devi became sullen. "It's not good to be always kidding. I am talking something serious; and you..." "OK OK. I am now serious. Tell me what you want to. Had any of our neighbours visited Canada? Why should they phone him? He rather would have called them.

He regularly talks with them; do you ever know it?"

"All right. Whether he calls them or they call him- the matter, after all. is the same. Why do you ramble so much? Talking meaningless things anywhere and everywhere." "What rambling?" Aditya babu got annoyed. "I can't yet decide whether I should convert our house into an orphanage or old age home. I had raised the matter in our club because they can give me the correct advice."

"Yes, that is the matter." Usha Devi told with surprise. "How did Bunu know about it? He is therefore in tension."

"Granpa, Granpa... I came... ha ha ha..." with a horse held in her two hands, Khusi came running, and jumped into Aditya babu's lap, and mumbled with a smile, "You know, Granpa Mama cautioned me not to come... I came here secretively... ha ha ha.?"

Aditya babu held Khusi for some time in his hands stretched away, and pampered. And then sat her in front of already arranged teddies of elephant and horse. Then she began to play with them to the accompaniment of her babble. After the play began, Aditya babu looked at his saddened wife, and started. "You know Usha! The world has become smaller, and along with it become smaller the people. Understood what Khusi told? A

God-like innocent child; hypocrisy and falsehood have not touched her. She has been forbidden to come and mix with me. Would she ever tell a lie?" Unable to understand anything, Usha Devi had sat there grief- stricken, as though a rare opportunity had slipped away from her fist. She again muttered, "Bunu told...." Aditya babu interrupted her with conspicuous irritation, "Listen Usha. He is born to me; I am not to him. Even though I don't speak anything, I know and understand everything. He is now flying in the sky; and, therefore, thinks, he would walk over the rain, build a castle over the clouds.

But he cannot understand that all one needs for life is soil; the soil, upon which he was born, learnt to walk, and grew up since his childhood. And one more thing; life cannot be lived alone with money; love affection, fellow feeling and intimacy of people around us is absolutely necessary for life. Without all this he may grow up like a huge tree, but there will be no flowers on that tree, no fruits, no fragrance, not even a secure nesting place for a little bird."

"Why do you give such a lecture, as if taking a class?" Usha Devi tried to hush up her husband with her shout just as she jumped off her chair with fear, apprehension and incertitude. "I know everything, Usha. You think I lie down in slumber, and you talk with your son safely on the other side of the closed door. Isn't it? Why, don't I ever wish to see my son daughter-in-law and grandson, and talk with them? Since you talk with them through the loudspeaker, I hear everything from behind the door. So all the plans of apartment, removing the tenant, even the plan to keep Khushi away from me- I know all the plans. Ha ha ha..."

Usha Devi stood there dumbfounded like a speechless statue. When she realised that the man who seems to be ignorant about everything actually knows everything, and has kept all that suppressed in his bosom, she kept looking at Aditya babu in such consternation as if she had never seen him. She was trying hard to hold back the tear glistening in the corners of her eyes. She was looking extremely pitiable.

"Listen Usha!" After moments of silence, Aditya babu looked at his wife with tender, placid and meaningful eyes; made her sit beside him on the bed, and tried to speak cleaning his already choked voice. "How many days are left now? Ask Bunu to keep patience, and wait for a few more days. All this will be his. I don't want to be a horse at the race course at this age, I rather wish to be a horse for Khusi. He of course has not come to that stage but he will certainly be able to understand everything in due time.

Thirst

Setting up his stall at a very short distance from the ticket-counter, the man had been shouting. Some seven or eight onlookers had ringed him. People getting down bus or hurrying to catch bus were throwing cursory glances at them. The congregation gradually increased like a colony of ants. The man now smoothened his hat, adjusted his spectacles on the nose with a push of his finger, and invited the onlookers in an emphatic voice, "Come here dear sisters and brothers, mothers and aunties, sirs and sahebs. come here..." It is not a new thing that hawkers keep doing their business at market places and fairs where a crowd throngs up. Scabies lotion, China torch, whistle, kids garment, each household article for Rs 10- hawkers of all such variety always wait for a crowd and begin their business. These people can mostly be seen at the bus stand, but this hawker seems a little different. His style of approach, his confidence attracted the onlookers, and surprised them, too.

"Please come here... come here." The hawker-in-hat multiplied the tempo of his voice, and challenged," If any gentleman, mother or sister can prove my mantra to be wrong, then I will

tonsure my head right here in public. Challenge, Challenge!"
He tightly clapped a couple of times in harmony with his words.??
He had not yet opened up his suitcase. Had only been handing
printed leaflets to enthusiastic onlookers. There was such detailed
information in the leaflet that it would startle, astonish, and brighten
one's eyes. The gist of the page-long article titled 'Significance
of the Mantra' is that there would be a guaranteed solution,
through Mantra, of social, financial and domestic problems.

The names of about a thousand people who had been
able to solve their most difficult problems after realizing the mantra,
and photographs of a few were printed on that leaflet. But the
problem is, the letters were so small and the photo in black
white were so small sized like a ludo-dice that neither could
they be read nor identified. The enthusiastic onlookers were
still trying to detect the names and photos of their acquaintances.

There was a condition on the applicability of the mantra.
One person can use it only once; it will not work the second
time. The problem has first to be uttered aloud, and exactly
after four seconds, the mantra has to be chanted twice with
eyes closed. There is a different mantra for each person, but
the procedure is always the same. There is also a provision for
illiterates and blinds. If they themselves whisper their problems
into the ears of this seller of the mantra, he can understand it.
And then, the mantra would automatically solve the problems.
An enthusiast who had been observing the man- in-hat, the first
visitor probably, enquired," Are you a sorcerer? Or an ascetic
from the Himalayas?" The eyes of the gentleman vibrated with
questions.

He wanted evidence. The man could be an impostor, a
cheat. Twenty rupees might go in vain. After questioning the
man, he looked at the people gathered on either side; and looking

into the eyes of people standing at his back, he smiled. The gathering expressed support with their nod. Similar questions were also boiling up in their mind. About sixty or seventy spectators had in the meanwhile gathered around that man-in-hat. Jostling through the crowd, a middle-aged man came to the front and asked him with a surprise, "Were not you there at Rourkela a fortnight ago?"

"Yes, I was there " The man humbly admitted, and questioned,

"Were you present there, Sir?"

"Yes. You had been distributing the mantra packets at Sector-IV. One of my friends had obtained it, but I could not. He telephoned that the mantra had worked well. You had distributed only twenty packets there. Are you going to repeat here the same? or give some more?" The man smiled, "Only for twenty people, and not more. Just see the leaflet, it is clearly written over there. This is not my business; but a social service; fruits of my long years of austere meditation, meant for the benefit of the society. Twenty rupees charged towards the packing. Even my travel expenses are not included in it." The spectators once again searched the leaflet. Yes, it was written towards the end - "for twenty people only, according to the choice of the servitors." The inquirer who had raised doubts a moment ago, chose not to question any more. He rather uttered in disappointment, "only twenty people!" "I had taken a mantra-packet from you at Baripada." Another spectator making his way to the front tried to share his experience. "I am surprised to meet you here by chance. Can I get one more packet, Sir? I was able to solve only one problem with that packet It didn't work even though I avidly chanted the mantra for the second time. I would be grateful if you gave me another packet."

The servitor looked at him meaningfully and politely said, "I will surely give if something is left. Please wait." The third beneficiary now surfaced from amidst the crowd. "Namaste, Sir. I had got a chance to meet at the Brahmapur hospital two months ago. Was able to get a packet. My stomach problem has vanished since then. I am a poor man, would be greatly benefited if I could get one more." Leaving aside the man-in-hat, people now surrounded these three persons. The enthusiasts wanted to hear from these persons and verify the truth since they already had experiences. How many hours does the mantra take to work? Is there any side effect if the mantra is pronounced wrongly? Can one eat non-veg? Can ladies chant the mantra during their periods? How should a small boy of four, who hasn't yet started studying apply it? Can the mantra be recorded and preserved for future use? Will we get our money back if the mantra does not work?...

The number of spectators gradually kept increasing, and along with it, the enthusiasm. The crowd was all ears for the sermonisation of those three experienced orators, as if listening to divine tales about the God. A number of travelers had in the meanwhile deferred their time of travel, and some had even cancelled their travel. Will such an opportunity come again? Buses will be coming and going, today's work can be done tomorrow or even the next day but who knows when will again the mantra-packet be available and where? It is therefore wise to cancel the trip. With an exhibition of such wisdom, about two hundred people gathered there were listening to the significance of the mantra. The servitor now announced, "The mantra- packets will be distributed in half-an-hour. All of you please get ready." People now began to jostle among-themselves.

There was heat of March. Fireballs were falling from the

sky even at 10 in the morning creating mirage on the roads. It would be safer to get home back after finishing all work by eleven. Humans, animals, vehicles - all were seething on the hot-pan-like- roads. Hot and dry wind pierced the body like needles. Everybody was desperate for a little shade and water. People began to jostle each other in front of the ticket counter no. 4 exactly at that hour. Without caring for the heat wave, hot-pan-like earth, sweat drops dripping from the hair, the foremost work was to put out the fire blazing inside the mind. The mantra-packet can definitely douse that flame, that too with a guarantee at only twenty rupees. The rate of jostle therefore rose up.

The news had somehow spread from one ear to the other just in an hour in this part of city-mantra-packet is sold with guarantee for only twenty rupees. All the rickshaw pullers, autorickshaw drivers, fruit vendors, hawkers, helpers, drivers, conductors had gathered there; along with them were considerable number of people who did not seem to be travelers or traders. It seemed from their getup that while going to office, they have diverted their route towards this bus stand.

When the jostle increased, the servitor announced, "Kindly queue up you all, gentlemen. I will proceed near you to hand over the mantra-packets, but whom I will choose-it is my liberty. Such is the order of my Guru." Some people were impressed with the suggestion while a few disapproved. It was an undignified matter for many to be standing in a queue. But if such sentiments are considered now, there will be more loss than gain. It is therefore better to stay up in the queue. And here, like the compartments of a goods train, the queue stretched even outside the gate, with hope and trust.

I had positioned myself at the front part of the queue. I had been watching everything from the beginning, and trying to manipulate the situation to stay in the number one position as the chance of getting a packet was greater there. But, alas! Fourteen persons were there ahead of me. I couldn't know where they appeared from. My eyes had been fixed on the man-in-hat . Cleverer people had perhaps known it earlier. However, I must wait and watch.

A boy of twelve or thirteen had stood just in my front. Quite a clever boy; works at hotel Tarini. Cleans the table, washes the dish, cuts vegetable, and attracts customer with his shout - "meals ready, cooked with pure cowghee... please step in.. only 40 rupees, papad is free." He was in a hurry but could not leave the queue. Conducting himself unstably, and occasionally spurting out tune of of song. "How old are you, dear?" I asked affectionately.

"Eighteen." He smiled

"Eighteen ! True?"

The boy could know that I doubted his age. So he kept looking ahead without ever turning towards me. His smiling face was overshadowed with displeasure and indignation. He looked at me from the corrners of his eyes in such a manner that as if he wanted to say, "Who are you to ask me my age?

Will I ever get the two square meals that I am now able to get if I speak the truth?" In an attempt to restore his trust, I put my hand on his shoulder and told him with a smile, "Are you getting scared, dear? I am not police. Ok, just tell me, what will you do with this mantra-packet?" Doubts were perhaps dispelled from the boy's mind. He smiled with a regained trust. It seemed when I looked into his eyes as if he had nestled eyeful of dreams in them.

"Oh no, I am sure that you are not a police. Do the police ever stand in a queue? Besides, you are standing behind me."

He paused and fondled two dogs whom he perhaps knew. They would come to him and get away having a sniff at him." They are my friends. Stay with us in our hotel."

"But, you didn't tell me what you would do with the mantra-packet!" I asked him again as I caressed his head. "Eczema has developed in the finger-joints in my palms and feet as a result of working with water. Here you can see. I will get rid of it; the disease troubles me a lot.

If I am cured, I can work better. The owner will be happy, and increase my salary. With more salary, I will savour sweetmeat and watch Bahubali movie. Yes, I will also buy shoes, not ragged ones like yours, but shiny ones. And then, travel by reclining on a luxury seat to enjoy fair in our village. I will no more have to soft-soap the bus conductor; will pay for the ticket." With these words, the boy sat down there to remove insects stuck on the body of those dogs.

I was carried away off my mind after listening to the boy's plans. A deep sigh came out shattering my bosom. Placing my hand of blessings on his head, I once again asked, "What is your name, dear?"

"This is Krish, and that one is Kalu. Good names, eh? I have christened them. Krish is a real hero. He would never let the stray cows, bulls or crows come near our hotel. But Kalu only keeps eating, and sleeps close to me. Always stays with me."

"But, tell me your name ! By what name are you called?" "My name?" the boy questioned himself and began to think. A bearded man, with sandalwood paste on his forehead, a garland of rudraksha around neck, and several crystal necklaces, who looked the flabby abbot of some muth rushed in breathlessly just at that time and kicked the boy as one would to a football,

"You rascal, sitting here! I have been looking for you in the entire bus stand since an hour. Already irritated me, you scoundrel! Get away quickly and fill water in the tub, clean the tables... going or not?" The man occupied the place as he dispossessed the boy. Complaints were voiced, "Come in the queue. Sir!"

"He is my own chap, Sir. I had made him stand here. Why do you worry so much? " The gentleman assessed the situation while counting the rudrakha beads, and smiled at me like a familiar man. His lips were partly visible as they were greatly covered with his beard. When he smiled, a little of his teeth made black and white by checking betel, and a slice of his tongue could be seen. Still smiling, he asked in order to remove his doubts and apprehensions, " I hear the mantra is working within seven days! That whole city now reverberates with the news. People came rushing with hired autorickshaws and enquired me as to where the mantra-packet would be available. Could I know about it otherwise? It's like darkness under the lamp, eh?"

"Yes, I also hear the same!" I looked along the queue that stretched like a snake, but could not get a glimpse of its tail The gentleman smiled in an attempt to begin the conversation, and asked, "What is your occupation, sir?" "I am a writer. "I replied with a smile. "No, no. your job? Where are you working? In which office?"

He asked emphatically. The gentleman was sure that all writers were job-holders. And only the people with some job are in the activity of writing, and can be called writers. So he looked at me with his inquisitive eyes and gaping mouth to get his doubts cleared. "Believe me; I am only a writer. No job or business, nor politics; I only write," I replied politely. The gentleman stared at me in such a way as if he had never come across such a rare species. Then tapping his forehead twice he recollected something, and said, "There is a magazine stall near my hotel. The owner of that stall is a friend of mine. People throng the stall in the evening. Poets and writers gather there in a rendezvous. Tea and snacks are enjoyed, and even occasional meals in my hotel. But no significant sale, he once reported. He would perhaps close the stall. After all expenses of electricity bill, stand fees, salary to the boy expenses at the rendezvous, and the like, he cannot save any money. As he is an M.A., he had opened this book stall with much enthusiasm, but now come to realize that books cannot make him meet his ends. Closing down the business of book, he would now open a fast food counter there, as he reported. That would definitely do well; guranteed." Taking pause for a moment, the gentleman resumed, "Don't mind, Sir. Shall I ask you one thing?

Are you able to manage your family being just a writer?" Then he minutely observed my uncared for beard, wrinkled shirt, my satchel, my shoes with three repairs, and must have assessed," Why would this writer have stood here in queue under scorching sun if everything-was going well?"

Now I asked the gentleman with a smile, "You are the owner of a hotel. Mustn't be having any scarcity: business must be going well. Does this sun not singe you?"

The man was now convinced that I was a trustworthy person with whom sorrows could be shared; I woulk not make fun of him. He now narrated as he would to an acquaintance, "Yes, the business goes on well. But mine is not a stall allotted by the municipality. I have only roofed the place with tarpauline to make it my hotel. The place is not mine either. It is a government land, but it has owners too. There are custodians of all the tarpaulin- stalls you see here. A number of murders have taken place here in this matter.

Leave all this, Sir. I pay a rent of Rs.4,000/- every month, Municipality officials often come and demolish my hotel. I have also to satisfy them. Water is free, but the electricity bill is Rs Rs.800/-. Extortionist fees to the local goons, donation of the Laxmipuja festival, monthly allowance to the police, expenses at friend circle, binge indulgence - only 2or3 thousand is saved after all this. Rs 500/ - to the mother of this rascal, and the rest sent to my children staying in village. You know it, Sir. What is the value of 2-3 thousand rupees in present times? I now need a stall of my own where I can do my business freely without any fear of these goons and scoundrels. I can admit my children in better schools, purchase better dress for them, and purchase a pair of gold bangles for my wife as she has since long been demanding."

The man now sighed deeply. Perhaps turned to reality back from his world of imagination. A smile once again bloomed on his lips, and waving his hand at a young man stood behind me he greeted him : "Jay Jaganath! You are here, brother!"

"Yes, brother, my owner has sent me here," the young man replied.

" It is for him, not me. Brother, we are mere helpers. our job is to wash the bus, tap on its door, and bear beating from the public. I was just getting home back from the night duty, the owner ordered to come and get a mantra-packet. Have been hanging around here for an hour."

"He is after all an owner. What problem does he have? Why didn't he himself come?" I questioned even though unsolicited. "What are you saying, Sir! The owners will come here! Smoking cigarettes sitting in the association office. He will go home after I hand over the packet.

"Does your owner have any problem with this bus?"

"Yes, Sir who doesn't have a problem, after all? These are skimpy owners, Sir. Run painted second-hand buses, but brag a lot. My employer, after all , he is; why should I speak against him? Since it in an old vehicle, it requires frequent repair. Costs one lakh if once taken to the garage. There was an embroil because of a recent accident. The driver hit a motorcyclist in order to save a bull. The biker had minor injuries , but the bike was broken. Our owner had agreed to give a new bike along with the medical expenses, but someone had phoned the police.

What a tension it was! Our bus didn't have insurance or fitness certificate. To escape from the clutches of police and RTO officials is just like escaping from the Yama himself. It required a lot of expense. Leave it, Sir; it is a matter of big shots. Our babu has given me in Rs.100/- to stand here. If the packet is availed early, I will go home taking some fish. There has not been any non-veg. food at home for over a month." The helper now told the most surprising thing." Am I alone here, Sir? There are about 25 helpers standing in this queue.

You can notice them; just have a look at the queue at your back. The owners have been waiting for them at the office." Taking note of the number of packet-aspirants, the servitor now made an announcement. "I will come near you after half-an hour; please keep patience." Even though the announcement disappointed the people, no one was willing to leave that place. It seemed as if everyone had been testing their patience with a firm resolve defiant of the scorching sun. When I felt a numbness in my legs, I informed the persons standing in my front and at my back about the problem, "If you permit me, I'll straighten any legs."

"Oh, yes please! We will also go one after the other when

you get back. Otherwise, outsiders will step in. You can go now; your place is secure here." With the friendship formed in this short duration, they took pity on my condition.

Getting away from the queue. I straightened my legs and arms, and moved towards the tea stall. Now the bus stand seemed to have stood in a queue. No, the word 'bus stand' would be an understatement; the entire city had rather queued up there. Representatives of almost all sects, castes, creeds, and financial condition had been waiting there in the queue when the servitor would come and solve in lieu of twenty rupees their insurmountable problem. I slowly moved towards the rear side of the queue lest an acquaintance could be spotted. And my goodness! I found one!

"Brother Sana! You are here! Came here leaving aside your mason work?" Sanabhai works as a mason under a contractor; special class contractor and a man of crores. Always busy with some project or the other. Sana didn't have any respite as a result. "Oh! It's not for me!" Sana bhai explained, "The contractor has paid me 1,000 rupees to get him a mantra packet which actually the Chief Engineer requires. Would he himself have come here? Handing me 1000 rupees, babu went off to the site of construction. It had already become a long queue when I reached. I spent two hundred rupees to get into the queue. "How you did it?" I was astonished.

"A rickshaw puller had stood here. I offered him two hundred rupees to leave me the place, and he agreed to leave." "He left! Poor fellow" I murmured with irritation on that unknown rickshaw puller.

"Yes, he left. How much could he have earned pulling his rickshaw the whole day? Could never earn 200 rupees. Auto rickshaws are crowding up; who cares for a rickshaw? So happy to pocket two hundred rupees at only 11 in the morning, he has since long got in the nearby liquor shop.

"The place serials in the queue are also sold?"

"See, I got it cheaply. Look at the rear side. The serial numbers are sold for Rs.500 and 1,000. Just look at the queue at my back. Close to me stands the driver of the minister; next to him the P.A. of a powerful bureaucrat; then the accountant of Chunnilal-the Jeweller;

I don't know the man standing next to him, and that tall man over there is the salesman of the Prime Builder - they all have stood here like gentlemen purchasing the serial numbers for their bosses. Just go and find, the people who were standing at the frontmost part of the queue are no more there, their serial number have already been sold twice. The price is higher there - there is a guarantee of getting a packet."

"OK, Sana bhai, why don't you take a mantra-packet for you? Don't you have any problem? Scarcity? Something unattained???"

Sana bhai smiled as he wiped away the sweat dripping from his head in this scorching heat, and said, My wage is 500 rupees; I am content with it. I first kept for me my wage from the 1000 rupees that the contractor had paid me. Paid 200 rupees to the rickshawpuller. How much left? Shall eat a mutton meal at the dhaba when I return. I shall offer the rest at worship of Lord Trinath in the evening. Got anything? ha ha ha..."

"Do you believe in this magic and sorcery, Sana bhai?"

"Listen; this is not a matter of belief or disbelief, but of having and not having. You have studied a lot but have very little knowledge about the worldly affairs. Can understand it in future. The scarcity is greater at higher levels of society than it is at the lower levels. People who have more money, honour and power have even greater thirst; the feeling of deprivation is even greater. Therefore this queue in the searching sun, this hustle- jostle, the sale of serial members. Hurry up and see... if your serial member is secure or has already been sold!"

Sana bhai was not highly educated, but he told such quintessential words of wisdom that I hurried back to the place of my serial number to verify it with my education-borne-wittiness.

And Lo! a stranger had encroached my place! "Sir, I had stood here previously. You can inquire these brothers standing in the front and at the back" I pleaded with the stranger. "No, no! we have not seen you before. This gentleman has stood here since long. You go away to the rear end." Outcried simultaneously the hotelier and the bus helper.

The Undying

Lord Shani has cast his sinister look on the Kaibalya colony for the last six months, it seems. The day Sukanti came to stay here on rent, most of the ladies and gentlemen feel like living in an abominable environment, as if a hideous, unsocial being has trespassed into a secure and dignified horizon. And, has been tarnishing the grandness of the colony. Consequently, pressure on me has been gradually mounting. When an ambience of worship flows out of the neighboring houses in the evening, a shattering scream spurts out of Sukanti's house - I'll die, maa... won't do it again.. spare me this time, maa.. She thrashes her five year old son so mercilessly that the pitiable imploration of the child would moisten the eyes of anyone who hears it. The Laxmis in the neighboring houses cannot offer their worship with concentration; lines of anger, hatred and annoyance appear on their foreheads even though their eyes are closed for worship. Creating louder sound with the worship-bells, they fervently wish - would this bitch die.

The day the child's wailing is not heard, Sukanti's fierce

shout rends the evening.. She yells so loudly that each word she utters becomes audible even up to the end of the colony. Without mentioning a name in particular, she chews out even the forefathers of some unseen victim of hers. She blurts out such abusive words about parents of the victim that one cannot bear to listen.

Salutes to her husband. What a patience! The poor fellow listens everything silently with his head down. Sukanti of course at times flings a portion of that lambaste towards her in-law's family, but the husband doesn't say even a word. It seem as if there is no blood in the veins of that man, it has turned ice-cold.

Exasperated with all this, the respectable members of the society often assemble to have a discussion. Just as people of all caste, creed and religion gather together in times of a national disaster, the residents of the Kaibalya colony congregate, ignoring their personal enmity, beyond the surveillance of the enemy, to find ways to get rid of the problem. Everybody here is rich-honourable- knowledgeable; no one is inferior to any other. As a result, there goes on a storming out of each one's capability. And a transitory rise in excitement and heat. Someone suggests to inform the police; another suggests to sue in the court of law; another says that gundas will settle everything if money is thrown; female gundas are also on tap these days. When such deliberation was once going on, Sukanti was going by that lane by her scooty, and paused for a while near the congregation. She swam her eyes across all who were present there. She could perhaps assess their capability, could decipher their purpose. As she moved her scooty forward she hooted to make everyone listen - I'll book everyone under section 375, pooh! That's all, and the intelligentsia gathered there suddenly went out of their wit with these words.

Everyone became still in the action they were with - cleaning the spectacles, yawning, trying to speak with a wide mouth, giving arguments with a pointed finger, rubbing own back, or adjusting one's loose pants... everybody stood still, as though in a painting, for some time till Sukanti's scooty disappeared at the bend of the lane. The complicity still stays at the level of a mere complicity, and pressure has been mounting on me. Respectable ladies have more complaints than the gentlemen have. They are of the opinion that if such a bawdy, coarse and nowhere girl lives in Kaibolya Society, then she will pollute the environment like a rotten betel leaf; what will our children learn from her? Women possess such a divine power which the men don't have. They are capable of seeing with this power such things that even the sun or the moon can't see. Their power of conjecturing is so strong and immense that they can narrate the present, past and future of a person even without seeing him. All women of course do not possess such a talent, but each of the women in the Kaibalya colony is gifted with that power. So they can collect information about sukanti even words down.

The kitty party shone more vibrantly that day with the unraveling of a mystery that Mrs. Padhi made there. Everybody's ears were drawn towards her mouth to listen the secret. The excitement, curiosity and eagerness that pumped up the members present cannot easily be described. That after all is the greatness of gossip about others. Mrs Padhi started," Listen! You know where she flies on her scooty with so much grooming ? A housemaid! Only a housemaid! Can you believe it ? But it is true."

"Yuch, a housemaid!" Eyes of about the twenty curious women including Mrs. Das, Mr. Mohanty, Panda auntie, Preeti bhabhi and Mrs. Patnaik widened in awe. Rosy bhabhi was so much surprised that her eyelids couldn't drop down for quite some time: She inched closer to Padhi bhabhi, and giving an affectionate tap on her muscular arm she tried to get her disbelief cleaned. "Are you sure, bhabhi ? I thought she did some job. One would guess from her figure and her style of speaking that she might be a home guard or a constable in the police department. What an emphatic walk! Straightforward words! What sort of language!" "Huh" ! Padhi bhabhi twisted her lips in disgust. "You know, how It was discovered? The lady whose house she works in at Kalinganagar is my bestie. I had asked her to arrange a maid for me; I'll dismiss the one who is presently working.

As she has been here for three years, she has started to be impudent; not keeping the phone away from ears, how would she work ! Dimple phoned me yesterday- maids are staying in your colony, why are searching here and there ? I first got annoyed by her words. I told her bluntly that only number one people lived in the Kaibalya Society. Is it a slum that maids would stay here! But when she described her appearance - tall, black, rides a scooty, has a hoarse voice like a man and, you know one thing, this swellhead trumpets that this one is her own house ! See, what a dare! And, know another thing?"...

As she suddenly remembered some important matter, she gave the issue a break, gestured at the audience to keep patience, and changed the topic - "Hey, Supriya! Just tighten the screw of this earring of mine. The jewelers like Swarnachuda has also started to cheat. Can anyone believe he charged 22,000 rupees for this tiny pair of tops ! I had earlier had the set of chains for these tops. However, I can bet that all jewelers are cheaters." Flashing a dissatisfied yet contented look in her eyes, and a smile in her lips, she swam her eyes across the audience, and displayed her ear towards Supriya madam. All eyes now centred on the earrings that had so far not been able to draw anyone's attention even though it had been dangling there from Padhi babhi's ears. 'Wow! How gorgeous!' Each of them now listened in a phased manner, like the refrain of some chorus, to the narrative of speciality of these earrings. And as they began to recount the memory of their anniversary gifts their husbands had presented, Padhi bhabi returned, without the slightest delay, to the previous issue. "Yes, she hadn't gone to the work four days ago. But Dimple would not relent; why should she?

She pays her money regularly, but what does this chick do? She charged her - you were absent for three days just recently on the plea of illness; how many days you fall ill in a month, eh? You A know what the chick replied ? - "I had gone to parlour for hair-dyeing; it caused infection..."

A grin filled the environment as the ladies heard the mention of parlour. Huh.. as if a beauty queen... Aishwarya..ha..haha. Each one elbowed the other with a smile, and caressed their hair as they gossiped. "You are so quiet, Rosy Apa!" someone said from behind. "You are so late today!" It was perhaps a curious question from Deepa. Rosy Apa had sat pensive in a corner. She now got an opportunity to mitigate her grief. She now started with her sullen face - "The old couple have come last evening; God knows when they will leave. You know it well how much tension it means when they come.

They would always chide me for something or the other - do it this way... don't do like that... what to tell about them... Yes, you were saying something about that chick! What an ill-mannered bitch she is! You know, what she said yesterday!" Ignoring the trouble caused by her aged in-laws, Apa now concentrated on the national disaster. Leaning the upper half of her body she now narrated...

"Matter of yesterday! Monday. You know, I go to temple every Monday. Had gone yesterday, too. I had never before seen her there. She had stood just in my front. There was a great rush. My legs pained due to standing for long, I have knee problem, as such. I asked her to budge a little. I told her gently, but did she spare me! She turned back and stared at me with wide eyes. She pushed my basket with her elbow and said - "Come in queue! why do you jostle? We have stood here for an hour!" Oh my God! Is it her mouth or a sharp knife!

'Really!' all of them expressed their shock. "She is not aware of you, Apa. She knows nothing about you. Why didn't you give her a slap just as you had done with that golguppawala the other day!

She could have known who you are!"

"Oh, leave it." Apa expressed her magnanimity, and said in a voice affecting forgiveness, "It is not wise to argue with lowly people. Or else, would I have spared her!" "You are right, Apa. Do they have

any sense of respect? you will only lose your dignity. Where is she, and where you are! You know another matter, Apa? You will go out of mind to hear it. Some people in our society are running after her. They are making her phone calls, and sending messages!" A lot of such gossips continued through the party even up to the gates of their houses when they got home back. There was an unwritten consensus among the ladies- 'If ever you see her with my hubby, or hear about it, do inform me soon. It is wise to stay alert before an impending danger.

Of course. I don't trust or give any importance to many statements of women, but as I reached home in the evening the other day, my wife asked a question that startled me.

-"What had you been tattling with that witch?"

-"Who? With whom? Which Watch?" - I asked with surprise.

-"Oho! Don't show me your lawyer's wit. I am also the daughter of a lawyer, ok! Confess it plainly; what had you been chatting?" I was really not able to guess anything from the words of my wife. In an attempt to lighten the situation, I said with a smile, "you are the proud daughter of a renowned lawyer of Odisha. All the lawyer-wit of your father has been infused in your mind from birth; am I not aware of this truth even after fifteen years of our marriage?

Have I ever, therefore, won in any quarrel between us? Victory is always yours."

-"Don't try to evade. Near Narayani Petrol Pump, at 11.20 in the morning. Is it untrue?" Wives often fire in the air for their security; this is not a new thing. But my wife fires a little more; and I only browse the paper silently at such hours. If I argue or drag the matter no one knows where it would lead.

-"I have seen with my own eyes that day - she smiled at you when we moved past her house! Isn't it? I had sat behind you, and you think I couldn't know anything!"

-"But, bring me a cup of tea first; you'll interrogate later?" I thought

her mind would be diverted while making tea, and so also the topic. And then there would be an order to bring grocery and vegetables from the market, just as it happened daily. But this time, before she ordered, I started on my own, "can't anymore consume potato or onion considering their increasing price. Better not to mention about pointed gourd, bitter gourd or spiny gourd. How will the common man manage with this sky soaring price? Won't it affect the middle class? The vegetable bag cannot become full even with five hundred rupees! What a time is it! What do you say, does it hurt or not?" I looked at her gaping, waiting for her opinion. Daughter of a seasoned lawyer - can she so easily be diverted? Keeping the cup on the tea- poy with a thump, she resumed with renewed energy, "Just tell me, when that witch chance comes across us, she walks gravely as if the granddaughter of the Governor, but why did she smile slyly as she saw you?"

Oh God! Save me. The fact is, once a matter enters the mind of wife, it doesn't exit until it travels through her head and heart to the digestive tract to be boiled up there. I do not know if Charak Samhita mentions a remedy for this type of malady. There is danger if you at all speak on such matters; if you do not speak, the danger is even greater ".

-"Er, She might not have smiled at me. Muse have smiled at you.

Who wouldn't wish to smile at beautiful women? She must have smiled at you. I had been driving looking straight at my front; how would I know if one smiled or wept on either side of the road?

You just say, how would I ?"

My theory perhaps appealed her. An aura of satisfaction suffused her face. But said with much hesitation, "Are you telling the truth?" And then handed me out a bag and a long list of vegetables.

Thank God! I was saved !

Sukanti didn't look that bad. The colour was of course slightly darkish, but her construction was surely attractive. No one would believe, by seeing her, that she was the mother of a five year old child. She is always careful about her hair style, cosmetics and clothes, when she goes out. Sprays on her body an enchanting deospray that the fragrance scatters along the way she rides her scooty. And just at such times, even the elderly men come out of their home, let alone the youngsters. A few retired persons and senior citizens would come out to the lanes exactly at that hour, and talk in an audibly louder voice - "Jena babu, won't winter be cool this year... Vaishnav babu, the D.A. is not increased this time... Raju babu, why can't we hear the voice of your grand-daughter.. See Prabhu babu, Children these days have become very arrogant." Coming together they would then whisper - "the lady who just passed by... she doesn't have a sense of humility. Let alone giving respect or salutation to elders, she doesn't even bend her head down. So many of us have stood here; and she went past us as if she had not noticed us!! No manners!

Prananath babu showed up at my residence early one morning. Anyone would be irritated with the kind of complaint he had brought. While coming home back at ten last evening, he noticed that there wasn't enough space for his vehicle to pass. A scooty was parked occupying a considerable portion of the road. The lane, as such, is not so wide; and his is an SUV. How so much he honked his vehicle, no one turned up to remove the scooty.

He got down greatly annoyed. When he had got near the scooty, the lady came out of her house. Babu was already under the influence of foreign liquor; added to it was the irritation of getting no response even after ten minutes of honking the vehicle - he spurted a few abusive words mixing Odia and English language which, if put in simple terms, means, "Is this one your father's road? Why don't you keep the scooty in your house, eh?" Sukanti first moved the scooty to a side; and after staring him from his top to toe she said in his masculine voice, "you could see only my scooty parked here on the road; bud how can't you see that car parked on the road all day and night? Go and tell such words to the owner of that car, if you have the guts!" It was as if Sukanti placed an open challenge before Prananath babu. His inebriation suddenly dropped down by about eighty percent.

He was struck with surprise. A mere maid servant; earning by working at others' houses, staying on rent in an outhouse, but answers back bluntly to the famous land broker Prananath Baliarsingh! He felt he should better trample this idiot lady along with her scooty under his vehicle. This won't be a big deal for him. He has snatched land from a number of land owners, and handed it to the builders.

Bodies of some stubborn ones who had resisted could not get be traced; a numbers of influential people who could not get land or flat even after paying money are crooning behind him like a dog. The four layered gold chain - looking like a rope- that hung from the neck down to his bosom, and the bracelet on his wrist indicate power, weight and efficiency. A number of women like this one will be thrown away in an instant even with a blow of his mouth. Still, she dares to speak with Baliarsingh looking straight into his eyes! And challenges! So much arrogance! He was trembling with anger, and could do anything at the moment. He once browsed his pocket, and stomping with audible sigh up to the scooty, he stared at her with the ferocity of a tiger The scared deer should now have got back inside her house; but she didn't budge an inch. She also stared into the eyes of the tiger with the unfazed and confident look of a cobra. There was no sign of her making a retreat. Something struck Baliarsingh that he came back.

Now, Prananath Babu's question to me - should such an arrogant and misbehaving woman live in the Kaibalya Society? This was the exasperation of the respectable men folk. All dignity and respectability of the women of the Kaibalya

society was once completely soiled only because of this lady...!
An incident - rather an accident-of some other day. Almost
all the ladies of the colony had congregated at Panda Babu's
residence on the occasion of the birthday of his grandson.
Attired in their best clothing and adorned with jewelry they
were all smiles when they reached the party at about seven in
the evening. Ruma bhabhi first began to whisper through the
crevices of her ruddy lips that mostly remained open, "You
know Lazie!. I had been to Babu's shop a couple of days ago
to buy some cosmetics. I suddenly noticed there that witch!
What would I say! She was clad in a Sambalpuri saree, exactly
like this one of yours.

It, of course, did not at all look good on her. She smiled
at me as if I was familiar to her. But I turned my face as if I had
not known her. You won't believe- she purchased bangles and
bindi exactly like the ones I had purchased. See her fashion-
sense! I must admit that whenever I see her, all my anger soars
from my toe to the top. One who should live in some obscure
slum has come to live with us in the Kaibalya colony! And wear
sarees and bangles exactly like ours!

H u h..."

Daisy became downhearted (Ruma bhabhi calls Daisy
fondly as Lasie) but promptly said, "Apa, my husband had brought
it from Sambalpur. An acquaintance of his had purchased it for
twelve thousand rupees from Krutartha Acharya's showroom,
and sent as a gift. Such sarees are not available here!"

-"Yes, that I know. Hers must be a duplicate one. Duplicates
of everything are available these days. See this necklace here,
and say if it is original or duplicate..." Apa changed the topic
consolingly, and, after a while, whispered a new discovery, "You
know, that witch is not at all married, I hear." A number of ears

were gradually drawn closer, and they all expressed their shock, surprise and disbelief...

-"Then what about this son, and husband of hers?' quizzed a respectable lady.

-"God knows. Leave it, why should we bother about such people. Just tell me, how much the construction of your new house progressed.." A surprising thing occurred while all this gossip was going on. Sukanti suddenly arrived there smilingly along with her son, and a gift-packet in hand. The whole of Panda-family, all the ladies and a few of the gentlemen who were present there were thunderstruck. Utterly dismayed, when everybody looked at Panda Babu, he looked at his wife, she looked at her son; and the son at his own son. Not a word came out of anybody's mouth. The drawing-cum-dining hall that reverberated moments ago with noise had suddenly turned mute, it seemed. As if, not a single human being was present there. Even the dropping of a needle could create a sound. But the mystery did not last long. When Anurup came running towards Sukantis son, led him up to the cake-table and announced - 'my best friend-Abhijit', it was clear that the boy was behind that mischievous act. He had invited his best friend right there at their school. He is a little innocent child, does he have any sense of honour and respectability. Frowning and turning their nose up at the incident, the guests were already feeling suffocated as if someone had lifted the lid of a sewerage tank nearby. As she could realise the situation, Sukanti told Panda Babu.

"Sir,I am going home as I have some urgent work. Kindly do drop my son near our house." And then she left the place. All honour and respectability of the ladies of the Kaibalya Society was narrowly saved that day. Mrs. Panda had of course to offer a lot of clarifications as a proof of her innocence. A small child, unaware of worldliness - with such considerations, the members of the Kaibalya Ladies Society were magnanimous enough to forgive the Panda family. But, the pressure kept mounting on me. I am the Working President of the Kaibalya Welfare Society. Untimely demise of the president last year at t he age of eighty increased my responsibility. When the empresses of homes are displeased, what else can the irate husbands do? So, the complaint before me is - ask the house owner to drive Sukanti away from the colony. The residents should have some distinctiveness in order to stay in a dignified colony like the Kaibalya. One should have some reputation; some solid footing. The majestic manors of the colony, built upon thirty plots accommodate fifty-five families including owners and tenants. Each of the families has a status, and respect in the society. Almost all are of a distinctive category. If one is a renowned businessman, then some other is a former administrative officer. The son of one is in the USA, whereas the daughter of another is studying in London.

Someone owns a couple of foreign cars, and another has three dogs of foreign breed. The wife of one wears diamond ear-pendant on her anniversary, while another goes on a foreign trip. One has had open heart surgery at a cost of five lakh rupees whereas another has a kidney transplant at eight lakh rupees. The son of one has become broad-minded by marrying a Bihari girl, while the daughter of another is in a live-in relationship for three years. One has not stepped in his house at village for the last thirty years, and another has turned his share of paternal land at village weedy displaying there a legal sanction in the form of a red flag lest his younger brother should enjoy the land. People living here have many such distinctiveness which proves their efficiency and sense of respect. Their dignity shines through all these matters. Sukanti does not have anything of this sort. Her presence therefore is a disgrace for the entire Kaibalya fraternity.

Initially I hoped that all this conflict would automatically subside. No one would find time in their busy life style to bother themselves with others' affairs. But the babus and memsaabs here are unrelenting ! Now I feel that there cannot be a solution to the problem if it is left unattended; some step need to be taken for its solution. I decided to go to Khordha the next day and discuss the matter with the owner of the house. I hope the owner would understand the problem, and find some way out. It is also an issue of my prestige to solve a problem of the Kaibalya society. I have the confidence that I shall be able to convince the owner using all my lawyer-tactics. I shall make him realise that the matter actually tarnishes his reputation and image. He after all is the owner of the house even though he is not staying there. If the house earns ill reputation, it also means the loss of dignity of the owner of the house. Apart from this, the outhouse also destroys the elegant look of the main building. Its demolition is absolutely necessary.

With a lot of such logics and suggestions in mind I started off with my bike at eight a.m. in the morning. Since the road was not much crowded in the morning, I would be able to come back in two hours, and attend the law court, I had planned. I had hardly been two or three hundred meters away from the Khandagiri square, when a lady asked for a lift. She even came to the front of my bike stretching her arm to stop me. I put a sudden brake with embarrassment, and was startled when I looked at her face. That was Sukanti! Oh my God!

Scared by her presence there, I was nervously looking hither and thither, but she had, in the meanwhile, saddled the pillion wrapping her chunri around her face. I never expected that such a mishap would suddenly befall me. I could not think what I should do at that moment. I moved my bike forward as though I was a machine, and began to chant silently the prayer of Lord Hanuman. So many vehicles were moving along the highway towards their determined destination, but it suddenly disappeared from my mind as to where I was going. Various evil thoughts crept into my mind. Many gentlemen have suffered humiliation, landed in trouble, and lost money only by giving lift to unknown ladies. My situation is even more horrible. Despite being the working president of the Kaibalya Society, I am moving with that lady at my back on my bike, for whom such a pandemonium has erupted in the society. This is just like inviting a trouble that was going along its own path on the highway. My throat turned dry in anxiety. O Lord Hanuman! Give some idea to this naive, O Lord!

Whenever I wear that lawyer's black coat, a lot of ideas and wisdom surge in my mind; the brain functions at lightning speed... but where is now that energy, wisdom, and speed! O Lord! May at least the news of this present picture not travel up to my house... Advocate Anand! You are now gone, O poor man...

My heart beat regained normalcy after ten minutes. Perspiration evaporated with wind. Mind gradually gathered strength. I have put helmet on head and she has covered almost whole of her face -who can recognise us in such getup? Taking opportunity of the situation, I applied sudden brake a few times, thinking that she would be strewn on my back, like a basket of flower; but alas! Keeping her hard bag between us, she had clutched the rear rod of the seat so firmly that she didn't budge even an inch. After a few moments when the road was a bit uncrowded, she brought her face closer to my ear, and said, "Can you recognise me, Kahna bhai ?"

My foot involuntarily pressed the brake lever: who could she be! She knows me so well; addresses me by my nickname of childhood days. Is Sukanti an acquaintance of mine but I cannot recognise! "I am the youngest daughter of Jagu Jena." She introduced herself once again bringing her mouth closer to my ear. The speed of my bike had by that time decreased to only twenty or thirty kilometers per hour.

Jagu Jena used to cultivate our farm land on contract. I have seen him since my childhood, and we siblings call him Jagu uncle! Since he had very little land of his own, he cultivated our land on contract so that he could sustain his family. Among his four children, the son was the eldest, and then the three daughters. Sukanti was the youngest one. She was only nine or ten when I left village. Eighteen years have passed in the meantime. I rarely go to village, my brother deals with all matters. All my calculation now proved wrong. I had stepped out to solve one problem, but now an even greater problem cropped up. Jagu uncle was the true provider of food to us. The land of course was ours; but it was he who raised and harvested crop with his hard labour. Not only he but also auntie and the children, even Sukanti.

She used to walk behind her father carrying a bundle of paddy crop from the land to our barnyard. If there is no crop to carry, there must be pitcher of water on her head. I stopped my bike at a roadside sweetshop and asked Sukanti to come for a cup of tea. She quietly fallowed me, we sat in a corner facing each other.. She unwrapped the chunri from her face and hung it on her neck, and I kept my helmet on a chair. I could not actually recognize her. There was a wart to the left of her nose, and I used to tease her for that and she would sob at my teasing. The wart has of course grown a bit larger, but it is not easily noticeable because of her dark complexion. She sat silent for some time until I asked her to tell something about her. Then she recounted for about fifteen minutes matters about the village, her family, the death of her father, her sister's marriage, and about her in-law's family. But she forgot to speak about her own life, it seemed.

"Well, what are you doing here? I mean -you are staying in Bhubaneswar; but where are you going this way?" She began to speak with caution. And asked, "wouldn't you mind, really?" Then narrated her long tale when I gave her an assurance. After two years of matriculating from the village school, she married; untimely death of father-in-law and mother-in-law in an accident; rift between the brothers and the birth of her son. Since her husband could not find permanent employment at village, they are here in Bhubaneswar since six years. "What kind of job are you doing here?" Although I had heard that she had been working as a housemaid, I wanted to be sure about it.

To wash dishes at other people's homes despite being a matriculate - It seemed to me a bit absurd. My asking her could not bring any change of reaction on her face as if I had asked a very unextraordinary question. There was no trace of shame, discomfiture or regret on her face, she rather began to narrate with extraordinary ease, "I first started working at a prawn factory, the job was to remove scales from the larger prawns which were then exported. About twenty-five ladies used to work there with regular, monthly wages. I had worked there for only a year when the factory closed because a woman died of a gas-leakage.

Pintu was born the next year... my husband was at that

time working under a mason. He was not able to find work every day. The Bihari ard Bengali labourers came to do the work at low wages; how would our people find work daily. If I don't go out to work, how can our family survive? After all, the expenses increased after birth of our son. Then I joined a printing press; paper- cutting and binding, the press also shut down when I had barely worked for a year. Everything is done through computer these days; how would human labourers find work? Then I started giving tuition to small children near my rented home in that slum, and continued for about one and a half year. But misfortune has been always following me. An English Medium Nursery school opened soon near the slum. Even though people live in slums, they all want to send their children to English Medium school.

How would any child then come to me for tuition?" Wonder-struck, I was only listening, and thinking: is this the same sobbing girl who used to walk with her little feet behind her father, carrying a water-pot on head? She keeps moving forward today,despite so much adversity, carrying the loads of her little world. "Bhai, take your tea; it is getting cold." Bringing me back to consciousness, she continued with her incomplete story- "Another problem cropped up after I was off with giving tuitions. I was stuck at home for three months without any work; and my husband began to suffer from stomach problems. Could not go to work every day. I suggested him to learn driving. There was no means to run the household. I do not like to beg help of anybody. So, I started working as a maid at three houses. It brought me three thousand rupees every month, and this much was quite a great thing for us at such a time. After working as a maid for seven months or so, I got a job at the Maa Bhagawati Cloth Store; working there for one and a half year. You might have heard name of the store. I get eight thousand rupees a month."

"Don't you ever face any problem ? I mean, all of your work... besides, you are a lady..." Even though I could not utter it, she could understand what I wanted to ask her; and she smiled. "Do you think that all the people in this world are honest like you? One incident had caused me intense pain when I was working at a house at Kalinganagar. The lady-owner of the house accused me as a thief. I of course quit working there, but I also blurted a lot at her before leaving the work. If I had the intention of stealing, I could have stolen costlier things; why would I steal onions?"

Onions! Ha ha ha ..I could not help laughing; nor could she.-

"The matter actually was not with onions"

"What else, then?"

"After Saab leaves for his office, memsaab engages herself unethically with a distant-cousin of hers. And, I once discovered them in such a situation - that I cannot say in front of you. After that I was branded as an onion-thief. She could have allowed me to continue working there if I had wheedled her; but why should I wheedle? I would speak straight forward all that I wish to speak. I do not know the art of whitewashing or flattery. A friend of mine had been working at that cloth store; she told the owner about me. I have been working there a week after I quit working at houses."

"Well, who else are staying with you here in Bhubaneswar?"

"My mother, my husband, son and I - we four are all."

"Oh, that's nice."

"Of course there are four, but I have to do almost all household work. My husband drives a private vehicle; often goes out on duty for a week. My mother lies ill-I have to attend her; have to drop my son at his school in the morning... a devil, he sometimes troubles me a lot; would surely have done some mischief by the time I return from work in the evening... broken a glass, or damaged the wall clock, or at least, would surely have emptied my talcum powder in his pencil-box... I slap him hard with anger... the poor boy cries a lot... a child, after all, he is..." Sukanti's eyes brimmed with tears. She looked vacantly down the road, a despondence clouding her face.

Motherliness and helplessness were teeming in her eyes seeking liberation; she controlled herself quite cautiously and turned somber. In an attempt to distract her from her somberness, I asked, "Your neighbours are quite a gentlefolk; how do you get along with them?" "Neighbours?" She spoke with a marked sarcasm in her voice. They might be richer than me, but none of them has a heart. They are even more mean in their mind. You might have known everything about them. After all, rich people have greater secrets. You will be surprised to hear about them from the maids working at their houses. Mohanty Babu's parents had come here. He did not let them stay here even for a week; left them at village. He spread a news that the old couple could not adjust here in the city. But the real thing is, if they stayed here, madam's status and vainglory would be diminished.

Das Babu is embroiled in a legal case with his younger brother to take his share from their paternal land. The poor brother is little educated, and had been making his both ends meet by cultivating the land... who else would you hear about... The two sons of Singh babu had been recently seen dragged into police station after taking drugs. If ever I smile at his wife, she would immediately turn her face away. Huh! as if wife of a crorepati ! Leave all this, bhai; would you ever call these people gentlefolk? I don't care for these people, their richness or their status. I toil, and manage my family. I am not showing off arrogance cutting others' throats, as they are doing. I don't care or fear them. Why should one who labours hard fear anyone? I am content with all I get. My principles are like my father's. Have you ever seen him swindle away even a palmful of paddy from your barnyard? Has he ever stolen gram or lentil while harvesting? He could manage his family of five, and live with dignity. Never begged or implored anyone for help. I am the daughter of such a man."

She told a lot many things in a short time. "Well, you would burst out laughing to hear another matter. The sons of Patnaik Babu and Dey Babu - they are much younger than me. Perhaps studying in college. They telephone me.. , and speak unsavoury things; give missed calls, and send such messages that I can't show to you. I secretly informed their parents about the matter, but they got furious at me. They told that, their children were very polite; they could never create such nuisance. I showed them my phone. They would still not believe it. After that, I thought of a plan. whenever they telephoned, I would come out to the lane and scold loudly looking at their house, so loudly that my abuses could be heard in their house. Then, there would be no phone call, missed call or messages for about a week."

She began to laugh as she said all this; nor could I help laughing out. "And, your house-owner... what type of man is he?" "My house-owner?" She had as if curiously been waiting for this question. A smile of joy beamed on her face. "Do you know who is the owner? It is Dhananjay Pradhain. The owner of our shop. Two more shops, like the Bhagawati Cloth Store, have now opened up at Cuttack and Balasore. A perfect gentleman. The house I stay now at had remained almost abandoned. He spent some money to get it repaired, and asked me to stay there, and take care of the house. Asked me to continue to stay here as long as I wished... Still, I pay one thousand rupees every month to his brother-in-law who has been managing everything about the house." A spontaneous smile of satisfaction spread on her lips. She quietly looked at me for some time. Then, arranged her chunri, and vanity, and got up. I was filled with surprise. Thought, she would ask me something, or would request for something. Or at the least, in the name of our relationship from the side of our village, would invite me to her home, or propose to visit our home in the colony. But she did not speak any such thing or make any request. A mysterious smile dangled from her lips ridiculing the entire gentle folk of the Kaibalya Society.

And the radiance effusing out of her eyes clearly indicated that how many times you might uproot and throw her away, she was steeped in a courage, confidence and strength to be rooted again and stand erect. "Where would you go, bhai?" Her curt question pushed me on to ever more surprise and embarrassment.

BLACK EAGLE BOOKS

www.blackeaglebooks.org
info@blackeaglebooks.org

Black Eagle Books, an independent publisher, was founded as
a nonprofit organization in April, 2019. It is our mission to
connect and engage the Indian diaspora and the world at large
with the best of works of world literature published on a
collaborative platform, with special emphasis on
foregrounding Contemporary Classics and New Writing.